"WHAT REASON NOW FOR ME TO HIDE MY LOVE?

" . . . for I do love you, Polly, with every breath I take. I thank God the truth has come to light before it's too late."

His arms were around her, his body lean and muscular. She clung to him enraptured as he brushed her face with his lips; and sighing, she felt contentment that was not to last long. The enormity of their behaviour made her push him abruptly away.

"Oh, Richard, what are we doing? In less than a week you will wed Arabella."

He laughed quietly at her soberness. "There will be no wedding. Don't you see the fate that lured you into that house was meant to be, my darling? Arabella will have no choice but to release me."

SWEET REVENGE

DOROTHY WAKELEY

Published in England as Remember Caroline Mary

C

CHARTER BOOKS, NEW YORK

SWEET REVENGE
Published in England as REMEMBER CAROLINE MARY

A Charter Book/published by arangement with
Robert Hale Limited

PRINTING HISTORY
Robert Hale Limited edition / 1983
Charter edition / June 1984

ISBN: 0-441-79122-0

Charter Books are published by The Berkley Publishing Group,
200 Madison Avenue, New York, New York 10016.
PRINTED IN THE UNITED STATES OF AMERICA

One

"And so you see, Mary Fielding, what a lucky young woman you are."

"Yes, Mr Ryman."

Polly stood for a moment overcome as she looked from Ryman to the splendid gentleman who was Arabella's father.

John Hamilton's eyes watched her closely and he sighed as if perplexed, yet his voice was reassuring. "Arabella has spoken well of you, my dear, and is anxious to see you established. Does the idea of living by the sea, sharing my daughter's company, please you?"

She could hardly find her voice as she whispered, "Oh, yes, sir," and stood rooted to the spot. The thought of leaving this discriminating school in Bath, where most of her life had been spent, caused her heart to beat wildly beneath the straight cotton gown.

"Well, get along," came the familiar voice of her master, "Don't fidget, girl. Pack up your chattels tonight and be ready to leave at dawn. Mr Hamilton's generosity will not tolerate a dawdler."

At the encouraging nod from Arabella's father Polly fled from the room and once in the corridor the cold stone stairs were taken two at a time. Fortunately, no one was in sight to reprimand such unseemly behaviour in a young woman approaching her eighteenth birthday.

Her impatient hand flung wide a door on the landing and she burst in upon Arabella Hamilton.

"Oh, something wonderful has happened," she cried flinging herself happily on to a bed. "Your father is here, Arabella, and I'm to travel home with you tomorrow. I simply can't believe it."

The other girl, scrutinising a pile of pretty underwear, glanced up calmly. "It's what I expected, Polly. Papa can be very persuasive when he likes."

"Then you know? It was all your doing? Oh, thank you, Arabella, I shall be eternally grateful." Polly paused, looking keenly at the other. "Do you find life so lonely in Devon that you need someone like me?"

"Not exactly, but Papa is full of benevolence and happy to pleasure my whims. Besides, I felt it time you left this dreary place. Was Mr Ryman put out?"

"It's difficult to tell but I'm quite sure your father's influence had effect. Earlier this afternoon when I was called into the office and given a lecture on behaviour and humility, I guessed there was something afoot."

Pursing her lips in an absurd imitation of her master, Polly aped cleverly. "Remember your place, Mary Fielding, be subservient as befits your station and thank the Lord for his mercy." Her mouth resumed its natural shape as she laughed. "I'm only addressed as Mary when he's being impressive. I've been Polly to everyone for years."

"Quite right too, Mary doesn't suit you at all. Don't give a thought to the hateful Ryman, he's been dependent on you for too long and, remember, we're never likely to set eyes on him again after tomorrow."

The two young women sitting side by side were

much of an age but there all similarity ended. Arabella
Hamilton had splendid dark eyes in a long, narrow
face topped with glossy black hair. There was a
natural confidence about her for, petted and
pampered, with flounces on her bed and blue ribbon
in her drawers, she was the school's most favoured
pupil. Her very antithesis was Polly Fielding, petite
and alive with quicksilver movements and abundant
vitality.

"Prepare everything tonight and don't oversleep,"
Arabella warned. "We shall be leaving at six."

Polly nodded and hurried to the little box under the
stairs where she slept on a hard iron bed. Girls in her
position were usually denied the privilege of mixing
with wealthy pupils and it said much for Arabella's
influence that a friendship was allowed to develop
between them. Polly prized this gift beyond price, for
she was a foundling and never allowed by her betters
to forget it. That she owed her place and education to
an unknown benefactor was fully understood, and
gratitude combined with a quick brain made her an
adept pupil. This combination was shrewdly used by
the schoolmaster, for Polly's latter years were spent in
tutoring younger girls. There was no resentment in
such exploitation, however, for she seized every
opportunity to study the manners and speech of well-
bred young ladies and soon her own irreproachable
behaviour surpassed many of those she admired.

From the day Arabella Hamilton arrived at the
school, miserably homesick and unhappy, Polly had
lent a sympathetic ear. She admired the faint delicacy
surrounding the tall girl's stately figure, her carefully
composed face and beautiful dark hair, and for years
Polly served her devotedly. She had dreaded
Arabella's approaching eighteenth birthday,

deploring her departure from the hated school, never
dreaming that she, too, would be shaking its dust from
her heels.

Now, sitting on her bed, the impact of such a
consequence left Polly breathless. No more rising at
six and supervising endless breakfasts, no more
teaching bored little girls their unwanted lessons. Her
world had turned completely upside down, and still in
a halcyon dream she began stuffing her pathetically
few belongings into a wicker valise. She looked around
her cell – for it was little more – without resentment.
There were times when privacy was welcomed, for here
the art of perfecting herself was secretly devised. In a
cracked mirror she practised dropping her eyes
discreetly and controlling a coquettish smile. A curtsy
or a bob to a gentleman was mastered with ease until
few qualms were felt at meeting nobility on equal
terms. A fierce determination to succeed in the new
life ahead, and exhilaration at escaping from
obscurity, possessed Polly.

Pushing a last kerchief into the hamper, she ran
impatient fingers through her short auburn curls.
Denied by her master the luxury of long tresses for
reasons never discovered, she hated the style which
made her look like a boy, and vowed to grow it as soon
as possible, hoping to disguise what vivid red glints the
close-cropped curls revealed. That these enhanced her
emerald-coloured eyes was never considered, there
was no place for vanity in Polly's life and she was
unaware of the magnetism her bright, affectionate
nature exuded.

While awaiting the sleep she believed would never
come, thoughts of an unknown future persisted. The
Hamiltons lived in a small seaside town in Devon
county, which brought fulfilment to another of Polly's

dreams. She had never in her life seen the sea or sniffed the fresh, tangy breezes so often read about in books. The vastness of it all and the ocean's restless rhythm had yet to be experienced and was awaited in great anticipation.

Instinct told her that Stoke House, presided over by widower John Hamilton, would house efficient servants and not lack luxury. But it also told her that a man with two sons for company was kindly disposed towards the needs of his only daughter.

Gazing through her tiny window at the moon, Polly felt grateful for the promise it held, grateful that she in all the world should be chosen to share the joys of Arabella's life.

The journey from Bath was long, necessitating a change of horses at Ilchester. Polly, aware of her scuffed slippers and shabby muslin gown drew the silk shawl Arabella had given her closely to disguise it. She was also aware of Mr Hamilton's discerning eyes, although, admittedly, after a few pleasantries, he made little conversation and was soon asleep. Arabella, too, drooped in the most surprising manner, but Polly was happy to let the dark head rest on her own shoulder, for the swaying coach failed to disturb her. Hungrily her green eyes darted about the countryside from Somerset to Devon, for never had she seen so many trees flaunting their new leaves on every gentle hill.

It was early evening when the carriage stopped before the steps of a large white house, and Arabella roused herself to straighten her bonnet and smooth her cream travelling-cloak. Polly, in spite of her earlier confidence, felt some apprehension, but John Hamilton handed her down with the courtesy shown

to his daughter before turning a beaming face to a
small group of people assembled on the steps. He
leaned to kiss a frail old lady who gave Polly a puzzled,
suspicious look, and he put his arm around a young
boy with dark eyes like Arabella's.

"My Aunt Sophia," a voice whispered in her ear,
"and my younger brother, Oliver."

The boy stepped forward and kissed Polly's hand
with such solemnity she had to suppress a quirk of
amusement, then they were suddenly surrounded by a
group of gaily chattering young women. Beautifully
dressed and twittering with excitement, they fussed
about Arabella, and Polly, ill at ease, turned and
looked tentatively across an open lawn. To her
amazement it ran straight to the sea. The sun on
gently rippling waves entranced her and engrossed in
wonder she wandered towards it forgetful of her
manners until the sound of her name was heard.
Flushing at her own discourtesy, she turned and saw
that two gentlemen riders in buckskin breeches and
elegant coats had joined the group by the steps. They
were conversing with the lively company while the boy
Oliver fed sugar lumps to the horses.

Arabella drew Polly forward and nervously she
looked up. Her bonnet slipped to the back of her head,
revealing curls touched to fire by the sun.

"A redhead, by Gad!" cried a male voice with
amusement. "What a welcome addition to town."

"Pay no heed to my brother's disgraceful manners,
Polly." Arabella laughed indulgently. "Hugo is noted
for his audacity."

Polly dipped a curtsy before the grinning horseman,
then her eyes slid to the other man. He sat straight
and proud on a great black gelding, and although his
eyes were hidden in shadow, instinct told her of his

gaze.

"Sir Richard Meredith," Arabella was saying with a peculiar lilt in her voice. "This is my friend Polly Fielding."

Polly acknowledged his curt nod but was watching the colour creep into Arabella's face and noting the look in her eyes as they rested on this fine gentleman. She made no comment and turned to pick up her valise. Politely, a servant's hand forestalled her and she realised how quickly such attentions must be accepted.

With some trepidation she followed the party entering the house. Large comfortable rooms with graceful furnishings and abundant flowers were glimpsed as ascending the stairs, her hand caressed the beautifully polished rail.

"I can't believe this is really happening to me," she whispered to Arabella, conscious of a trim maid within hearing.

"You'll soon get used to us all," came the reassuring reply. "Don't bother to change for supper – and Polly – " Arabella hesitated: – "Hugo is not as insolent as he seems, he just can't resist teasing."

Polly's heart immediately lifted.

"Will everyone be staying to supper?" she asked.

"You make them sound like an army," came the laughing reply. "Sarah, Clarissa and Lucy might do that, they spend a deal of time here."

"I see. Does that include Sir Richard?"

Arabella blushed at the teasing question. "He doesn't visit as often as we'd like and, strictly, is not Hugo's type at all. But his stables at Budleigh are the envy of Devon county and many people forgive his taciturn manner simply to take advantage of his stock."

Arabella was obviously trying to keep her voice firm but a quiver of excitement betrayed her and Polly guessed the joy of returning home had affected her deeply.

The supper table, sparkling with silver and crystal, held the most delicious food, and eating heartily Polly covertly surveyed the company. Several times she found the eyes of Mr Hamilton disconcerting, and nervously she felt he might be contemplating with misgivings Arabella's whim. Sarah Caldwell dominated much of the feminine conversation. She and her sister Clarissa pointedly ignored Polly and this superior conduct seemed to annoy Lucy Carmichael, whose face beamed at Polly with friendly approval.

All the girls wore fashionable flimsy dresses of the most delicate colours, and Arabella in lilac silk, her dark hair twisted with ribbons, filled Polly with envy, and she was conscious of her own gown, creased and travel-stained.

Sir Richard Meredith, to Arabella's obvious satisfaction, had consented to join them and sitting next to a shyly silent Oliver was the elderly aunt. Old-fashioned feathers danced on her head when with eccentric abruptness she disturbed the pleasant chit-chat at the table by barking a question directly to Polly.

"What brings you into our house as a permanent guest, miss?"

Although taken aback, Polly immediately went on the defensive, a role she had often taken before.

"Because Mr Hamilton invited me, madam. I'm to be a companion for Arabella."

"A likely tale, the girl has enough friends."

At the sight of three other females, all obviously on

intimate terms with everyone present, Polly felt inclined to agree but, feeling her colour rising, she glanced quickly from face to face. Grins of delight, Arabella's frown and Mr Hamilton's unconcern were evident, as was the look of faint interest in Richard Meredith's eyes.

"Behave yourself, Aunt Sophia, please," Arabella bade reprovingly.

"Can't the wench speak for herself?"

"Certainly I can," Polly answered quickly. "And forgive me for saying it is none of your business, madam."

"Good for you!" Hugo applauded loudly. "I can see mealtimes in future being greatly improved."

For some reason Polly felt his remarks out of place but the fleeting look of approval from Sir Richard was gratifying and suddenly the goodwill of this silent man became important to her.

Important enough to instil ambitions never before considered, and the longing to enter this unfamiliar world of superior people was intoxicating. She already had the affection of Arabella and she hoped the respect of Mr Hamilton. As for Hugo and the disagreeable Aunt Sophia, a fig for them both!

Leaving the gentlemen to their port, Arabella later led the way to the drawing-room decorated in green and gold. Polly, her eyes wide at such opulence, sat shyly on a little gilt chair, but Arabella would have none of this and pulled her towards the other girls.

"Polly has never lived in a house before and I wish her to become one of us."

"Do you mean she's lived in the middle of a field?" Sarah Caldwell asked with sly innocence.

Clarissa laughed but Lucy Carmichael snapped quickly, "Don't be so facetious, you know perfectly well Polly was at Arabella's school in Bath. I think we are fortunate to have a new face in our circle."

"Of course we are, Lucy. Did you ever see such a pretty little thing?" Arabella asked sweetly.

"Not more than five feet, I'll be bound, and her eyes are most unusual. But the hair's a bit startling, don't you think?"

"It will grow – we shall see to that – and, of course, a new wardrobe is promised. Come, Polly, have you lost your tongue?"

The slight figure scrutinised by three pairs of inquisitive eyes began to shake with fury. How dare they criticise her in such a high-handed manner as if she were a doll newly purchased.

"I would thank you all to treat me with a little more respect," she snapped icily. "Were my own manners so appalling, I'd be ashamed."

The silence that met her explosion was full of astonishment and Arabella broke it with acrimony. "Polly, you must refrain from such childishness – our remarks were well meant."

Lucy Carmichael put a friendly arm about Polly's shaking shoulders. She was a tall girl with kind but angular features. "Oh, yes, they were indeed. You've no idea how much I envy your dainty figure and the gold in your hair."

Flushing now at her outburst Polly looked with uncertainty at the surrounding faces. Arabella wore the bland expression she knew so well, but the alarm in the Caldwell sisters' eyes brought faint satisfaction.

"Forgive me, please," she murmured. "I was wrong to insult your guests, Arabella."

"Well, such a handsome apology cannot be ignored. You will find the courtesy taught at school often lacking here, Polly, and there is much to learn. But I admire your spirit and feel you also dealt efficiently with Aunt Sophia at supper. Only her age and feeble brain excuse her."

"Isn't it strange how the elderly are so easily forgiven. I wonder if we shall ever deteriorate to such a condition," Clarissa wondered, shuddering.

"Very likely," her sister replied, good temper restored. "We have a few odd characters in the district, Lady Regina Meredith among them."

"Polly is unlikely to meet such a frightening scarecrow. She hasn't been seen outside the Manor for years."

"Meredith? Is she related to Sir Richard?" Polly asked.

"His aunt, and a more uncivil, sour old harridan one could never meet."

"Richard's devoted to her, though. Don't forget she's the only family he's ever known."

"But such rumours about her and the former Prince of Wales, how can they possibly be true? At last year's ball she looked ridiculously fat."

"Well, so is the King, remember. Very likely she was one of his early loves."

"Does Richard ever talk about Lady Regina, Arabella? You know him better than most of us."

Flattered, the dark girl nodded with pleasure. "I believe I do, but there are more important things to discuss than his aunt. We kept in touch, of course, when I was at school."

"You mean he actually wrote letters to you?"

"Not with great regularity, but the occasional note was received."

Polly looked at Arabella in surprise. To her knowledge few letters, apart from family ones, had ever been received.

"You all seem extremely interested in Sir Richard Meredith," she said impulsively. "Is there something special about him?"

"I suppose there is," replied Lucy. "You'll soon learn what a scarcity of gentlemen abounds in this county. Apart from Hugo, who loves all and is faithful to none, Richard is the only presentable male for miles."

"I presume he resides with the peculiar aunt you were discussing."

"He does indeed, just five miles along the cliff. St Mary's Manor has been the Merediths' home for generations. Richard is now the sole heir."

"That sounds intriguing. Am I allowed the full story."

"Why ever not, it's common knowledge. You tell it, Arabella."

With her eyebrows drawn together in a slight frown, the answer came soberly. "There's little to tell really, and I do wish you'd refrain from treating gossip with such avid curiosity, Lucy."

"Don't be such an affected goose, we are all aware your ambition is to reign at the Manor one day."

"I'd never accept such an offer while Lady Regina lives. Life there would be complete misery."

"Has he spoken yet?" Clarissa asked, her eyes shining eagerly.

Arabella blushed. "Of course not, but now I am permanently here I hope a deal of time will be spent together. Such matters need serious consideration, you know."

Polly sat silent. It crossed her mind that if Arabella was truly contemplating marriage, how ineffectual was her own position. She also found puzzling Arabella's need for a companion while so many engaging girls claimed her friendship.

The cool grey eyes of Sir Richard were recalled and the urge to learn more of him was irresistible. She suppressed the dart of envy for the confident Arabella, and asked "May I hear more about St Mary's Manor?"

"As Arabella seems determined to concentrate on its lordly inmate," Lucy laughed, "I suppose you must learn the facts from me. St Mary's is the most beautiful mansion, standing high on the clifftop facing the sea."

"But cold," Sarah shuddered, "and slightly sinister. I hope when Arabella marries Sir Richard some changes will be made."

Ignoring the interruption, Lucy continued. "Lady Regina is the sister of Richard's father. Their parents died early and Ambrose succeeded to the title when he was only fourteen. Although Regina was years older than her brother, she had little control over him and at an early age his reputation as a reckless libertine became the talk of the county. You must understand that the rumours multiplied alarmingly but it was generally accepted that the conduct of Regina matched her brother's. Much of their time was spent in London, of course."

"The Court set was notorious in those days, hence Regina's connection with the Prince," said Clarissa.

"The gay life they led soon depleted a fortune and Ambrose eventually married a wealthy heiress with promises to reform. I doubt his word was worth a farthing but the newly-marrieds returned to St Mary's Manor and dwelt there until Richard was born. Unfortunately, the young wife died, leaving a defenceless baby."

"How very sad," murmured Polly.

"I don't think it bothered the child overmuch, but Regina took it to heart. Whether the Prince's favour was diminishing or Court life beginning to pall is unknown, but she deserted London to rear the child in surroundings more fitting."

"There was no lack of education, of course, with, I believe, a promised post at St James to follow," murmured Arabella, "but Richard would have none of it; after Oxford he came home to Devon."

"No wonder he adores Lady Regina. She's been like a mother to him."

"Well, naturally, but he's long past being dependent on such a tiresome old woman."

"What happened to his father?" Polly asked curiously.

"Oh, he forsook them both for the pleasures of London, coming back only periodically. The shady side of his life is seldom discussed, although heaven knows enough rakes abound even now to despoil our pure little bodies had they the chance. I believe Ambrose caused havoc among the local belles and when Richard was about ten – "

"Lucy! I really don't think you know where fact and fiction meet," Arabella checked the other girl. "We all know the facts you've just revealed, there can be nothing else."

Round-eyed, the other girls stared at a sparkling Lucy.

"Sorry," she grinned, "I get carried away."

"Don't stop" begged a disappointed voice, "what other secrets can you tell?"

The sound of voices and steps ascending the stairs put an end to their discussion, and Polly, although as curious as the others, felt a certain relief when the gentleman in question appeared. She looked at Sir

Richard Meredith with new eyes and turned away
flushing when his glance met hers. How would he feel
did he know his personal life had been bandied about
by a gaggle of girls? Times might be promiscuous but
a mere few hours had shown how mischievous the
tongues of her own sex could wag, but humility and
modesty would not be denied and she burned with
shame and a strange feeling of disloyalty.

Two

Upstairs in the room allocated to her, Polly put away
her things, a change of underwear, shoes and one
serviceable gown. Folding the shawl, Arabella's gift,
with care she inspected with delight her new domain.

Unaccustomed to sprigged quilts and rose-painted
water-bowls, she touched them timidly while glancing
at her reflection in the handsome mirror. Was it really
she, Polly Fielding, penniless and unloved,
experiencing such undeserved delights. Would she
awake in her stark little cell to find it all an impossible
dream?

But the chatter of the evening was far too vivid for
fantasy, whirling around her brain to make sleep quite
impossible. She slipped a bolt on her window and
stood on a small balcony, listening to the strange
sounds of the sea. Urgently it called her and without
thought her feet ran lightly down narrow steps into the
garden below.

In no time at all she had flown across the pebbles
and stood on the soft wet sand where the foam-tipped

waves, silver in the moonlight, begged for her touch. She felt so happy, happier than she had ever felt in her life as the rushing water lapped her ankles and, oblivious of a soaking gown, she crouched to let the sea ripple over her hands. In sheer delight she laughed aloud, then suddenly fell silent, for the sight of a horse soundlessly travelling towards her was frightening. Feathers of spray showered into the air, white-flecked and beautiful, and she thought that indeed it must be a phantom.

But the rhythmic gallop was solid enough and the rider reined his magnificent black horse beside her quivering figure.

"Well, well, little Miss Fielding," he exclaimed in surprise. "I hardly expected to find you playing on the shore at such an hour."

Fighting her confusion she faced him boldly. "Nor I you, sir. Is it a habit of yours to ride the night like a fury?"

"A bad habit, I'll admit. I've chased the devil out of Hell all the way from Budleigh!"

"Exactly how far is that?"

"Five miles west, there's no prettier place in Devon."

As he looked at her he thought she might have passed as a sea sprite, tiny and fragile, tossed up by the tide, and glancing at her little wet feet, he lifted her on to his steed with a swift movement.

There had been few animals in Polly's life. A nodding acquaintance with the Carter's docile mare, cows and the busy shires on scattered farms around Bath was the limit of her experience. This splendid beast, as strong and virile as his master, terrified her but never would she show it, and clutching the hard saddle firmly, she fixed her thoughts on the silent man now leading her along the sands.

"What brings you down to the shore?" was his sudden abrupt enquiry.

"The sound of it, sir. I've never seen or heard so fascinating a sight before."

"You'll have your fill before long, I dare say, Stoke House is but a stone's throw."

He stopped the horse and turning, looked up into her face.

"Sophia's words had a ring of truth; a companion for Arabella is nonsensical. How did it come about?"

"We were friends at school, you see, and I shall always be indebted to the Hamiltons for providing me with a home."

"You have none of your own, then?"

A shake of her bare head set the red curls dancing.

"I am a foundling, educated by an unknown benefactor and I simply can't believe the good fortune that brought me here."

He was rubbing the horse's silky flank gently, fully aware of her nervousness but her straight back of courage and natural dignity pleased him. He spoke to her quietly, pointing out visible landmarks until he felt the childlike figure relax, and unusual warmth flowed through him.

Her embarrassment gone, she now conversed freely with the man so lately a topic of conversation, but soon, aware this illicit meeting was slightly scandalous, she suggested they return to Stoke House. The strict protocol learned at school had made her aware of such unseemly situations, but if he considered her behaviour forward he made no sign.

"You must think me lacking in good manners, Sir," she murmured apologetically.

"Nonsense, child," came his reply with a flash of

white teeth. "I find you delightfully refreshing; decorum is of no matter to me. But do stop addressing me as 'sir'."

"Certainly I will if you stop calling me 'child'. I shall be eighteen years old in a few months."

"Almost a matron, I do declare!"

He caught the sparkle in her eyes as he swung her from the saddle with strong, firm hands.

"Such a little thing to be loitering at this hour. I'll swear no Hamilton is aware of this jaunt."

Polly's eyes flew wide in alarm. "Oh, goodness, no! Promise you won't tell."

"How could I betray so charming a lady? Now, to bed with you, Miss Fielding."

He watched her climb the cliffpath where she turned to see him cantering along the beach until a cloud passed over the moon. She remembered with pleasure his slow, intent smile, surely a rare thing bestowed only on those he favoured. Without vanity she counted herself among them.

The following morning was perfect, a brilliant sun rising rapidly to shimmer over the sea. Polly, free now of last night's timidity, entered the breakfast room to collide with a jaunty Hugo.

"Down so early, my little waif?" he asked with amusement. "Did you fail to rest in such unaccustomed splendour?"

She gave him a quick suspicious glance, feeling his tone insolent, but answered calmly enough "I slept very well, thank you. It's easy enough to accept comfort when the offer is gracious."

He barred her way and putting his hand beneath her chin, lifted her head to meet his gaze. "Not lacking in spirit, I see, but I trust you are not impertinent or rising above your station."

Polly moved quickly away, but catching her by the shoulder, he laughed in her face. "I think we shall find much in common, Miss Fielding. I have a fancy for redheads, you know."

Absurdly she felt her anger rising and began to struggle in his grip. "Kindly release me, sir, you are hurting."

His hands tightened, and she felt herself imprisoned as his face came closer to hers and suddenly he kissed her hard and long on the mouth.

Totally ignorant of the art of kissing, Polly found it far from being the romantic sensation she'd imagined and she tried to wrench herself away. He released her with such abruptness she staggered, but in spite of a rapid heartbeat her voice remained firm.

"Don't dare to take such liberties again, sir, my favours are not given lightly, whatever you think of my position in your father's house."

"I fancy you've never been fondled before," he grinned, "but I feel you'd make an apt pupil, begad."

"I think not, I find your attitude offensive."

"Polly!" Arabella's voice was sharp as she entered the room, looking fresh and dainty in a white sprigged gown.

"I do wish, Polly dear" she said, frowning slightly, "you had come to my room before rushing down to breakfast."

The other's green eyes flew wide. "Oh, Arabella, I'm so sorry. Should I have?"

"A little more thought for me might have been kinder, but no matter. Has Hugo been bullying you?"

"Of course not, idiot," her brother laughed into his sister's now smiling face.

Her friend's reprimand brought a small cloud to

Polly's horizon. She had not supposed Arabella
needed her services so early, certainly no such request
had been previously made, but vowing to be more
alert in future and not allow the novelty of her new
surroundings to take precedence over her duties, she
sat in subdued silence. So many bewildering events
had happened and it had not yet been made clear
exactly what her duties entailed. But if assistance with
Arabella's toilet was required, she was happy to
comply and had she done so this morning that
unpleasant scene with Hugo could have been avoided.
Her face still burned at the thought of those distasteful
kisses. Admittedly, his good looks were appealing and
possibly many girls were bewitched by his seductive
eyes, but there was no attraction there for her. That
Arabella found no fault in her brother was clear. It
was more than likely his capricious ways were
accepted without question.

Polly was no tittle-tattle, but the sharp lesson so
timely learned had taught her to avoid future brushes
with the conceited Hugo. She felt a little deflated and
the eager anticipation of revealing last night's
moonlight adventure to Arabella was momentarily
quelled.

When, after breakfast, brother and sister wandered
away together, Polly wondered if that impudent
gentleman was due for a scolding. Had she overheard
the discussion between them, however, great would
have been her surprise.

"You really are a stupid oaf. Papa distinctly asked
Polly be treated kindly."

"Oh, balderdash! I was only fooling with the wench,
she's mighty pretty, Arabella."

"That's as may be, but watch your behaviour.
Papa's particularly touchy on the subject – not that

Polly's likely to complain to him.''

Hugo plucked at his stock-pin irritably. "It's deuced odd having the penniless chit thrust upon us without reason, but I'm damned if I'll bow to her.''

"No one is asking for that, but she's surely not objectionable.''

"She didn't take kindly to fondling but I disbelieve in this day and age such innocence exists. However, no matter, next time I'll be more discreet.''

"Hugo! I've warned you about philandering – ''

"All right, keep calm, I'll preserve your precious Polly.'' He grinned suddenly and coaxed, "Come on, Arabella, you must know what's behind Papa's manoeuvres. All this fiddle-faddle about a companion for you is ludicrous.''

"Truthfully Hugo, with friends aplenty I've no idea why Polly was brought here. But naturally she'll have her uses, I've no intention of keeping her idle, a sense of proportion must be kept, after all. But please take note of my warning.''

Her brother grunted. "I hope the secret's revealed before long, for patience is not my greatest virtue, as you very well know.''

Later the girls walked into the charming little town where abundant shops displayed ample goods. Feathers and lace and coloured silks set Polly's eyes dancing and she was overwhelmed by Arabella's insistence on purchasing for her dainty materials and trifles of taste. They rested in a fashionable coffee house where several young people joined them. Sarah Caldwell's voice was clearly audible and Polly stood quietly aside while greetings were exchanged. To a casual observer their chatter would have been amusing but Polly flushed as whispered remarks turned curious eyes her way. After a while Arabella summoned her languidly to proceed to Stoke House for the carriage.

"But, Arabella, it's no step at all," protested an astonished Polly.

"I do wish you'd refrain from questioning my wishes; please do as I ask. You may be strong as a mule, Polly dear, but personally I'm completely exhausted."

Meekly Polly apologised, looking so crestfallen that she was patted good-humouredly. "Don't get into a pet, there's nothing wrong, I'm simply disgracefully lazy I suppose."

"I'll gladly come with you," a cheerful voice intervened and Lucy Carmichael, her freckled face beaming, linked her arm through Polly's.

"How very kind of you" Polly murmured as they walked up the hill together.

"Fiddlesticks! I find their continuous prattle intensely boring and the fuss being made of Arabella is quite absurd."

Polly stiffened. "Don't you care for Arabella?"

"Of course I do, but I've known her for years and feel entitled to criticise when I feel like it."

Polly made no comment and Lucy continued. "Hospitality at Stoke House is famed around here and I do hope your stay is a long one."

"I hope so too."

Polly glanced at the tall, thin girl by her side. By no stretch of imagination could she be called a beauty but her clothes were the height of fashion. Her yellow French bonnet, classical gown and pointed slippers had style and she wore them with ease. The slight shyness felt by Polly soon disappeared as the other girl coaxed her to talk.

"Well, in my opinion, Arabella's fortunate to have

you," Lucy murmured at last enviously. "I've seen a few companions in my time but no one remotely like you. I do hope we can be friends."

Polly's heart warmed to the other as they laughed together and later she revealed her enthusiasm to Arabella.

"Oh, Lucy's energy tires me," was the indifferent reply. "She comes from over the hill and apart from the Merediths her people own more land than anyone else around here. Lucy is an only child and very wealthy in her own right."

"But she has no airs at all."

"Rich people are usually unpretentious, you'll find, but in spite of her money there are few beaux interested in Lucy."

"Oh, Arabella!"

"It's true, I'm afraid. She acts like a hoyden and has little finesse. The Caldwell girls are much more popular, their good looks without exception. They will both marry well one day."

"I do believe you're a matchmaker at heart."

"But, my dear Polly, of course. The most exciting thing in life is finding a husband. I had hoped to match Sarah with Hugo but the high ideals of my brother will only be suited by an heiress."

Polly stared dumbfounded at the other girl, realising her life spent among refined young ladies had taught her little about their calculating minds. Naturally every girl dreamed of a successful marriage but elaborate manoeuvres to ensnare unsuspecting males seemed quite undesirable.

"There's much you have to learn about Society," Arabella continued. "A London season is commendable but I must admit everything at the moment is stalemate. All gaiety in the capital has been abandoned because of the King's health."

"When things are normal again will you have a London season, Arabella?"

"Possibly, but there really is no need. I feel my plans are developing quite satisfactorily here; we must wait and see."

Polly sat expectantly but it was obvious Arabella intended making no further comment and they were both distracted by the arrival of a seamstress to commence their new creations.

The discarding of her despised school clothing gave Polly satisfaction and although never before owning a decent gown, she had not failed to notice the simple elegance of the ladies of Bath with their classical styles. Although Arabella deplored her intention of copying that simplicity when this year's vogue was for enormous sleeves and flounces, Polly would not be dissuaded. Long Grecian folds gave an illusion of height and it pleased her to find a new dignity which even Hugo remarked upon.

The early June days of 1830 were peaceful and ones Polly was to remember with nostalgia. Kindness and consideration were received from everyone and even Hugo's crafty insolence failed to disturb her. John Hamilton's unexpected concern for her happiness was gratifying, too.

"I realise my daughter's pleasures do not include walking, and you, I understand, have a fondness for the sea. While not wishing to deny your pleasure, it would please me would you stay close to the house."

"Certainly, if you wish, Mr Hamilton," she answered meekly, "but Lucy Carmichael has offered her company. She, too, loves the sea."

He nodded approvingly and guiltily Polly thought of her sojourns at night to the lonely beach. If Mr

Hamilton became aware of her deceit, no doubt there would be trouble, and only the hope of glimpsing a handsome rider made the practice worth while. Such hopes remained unsatisfied, however, for Sir Richard's general absence was noticeable.

"He leads a busy life and at times is absent for months," was the answer to her query. "Something to do with his bloodstock, I believe. Why do you ask?"

"Just an idle question; he seems an interesting man and I fancy you care for him, Arabella."

"Really, Polly, at times you are quite impertinent. You must break yourself of such a deplorable habit."

The rebuke left Polly considering the other girl thoughtfully. There were many surprising things she was discovering about Arabella. In spite of her affability, at times her mouth set in the most alarming manner and if Polly failed to jump to obey her, complaints usually followed. Endless small errands were performed, retrieving books or fans from the garden, threading ribbons through underwear, arranging flowers and playing baccarat while the other reclined in pettish languor. As the weather became hotter Arabella developed a reluctance to leave the house and sometimes, although performing the tasks requested with good grace, Polly felt trapped. The times her friend appeared her former self, chatting idly and exchanging confidences, became rarer and her unpredictable outbursts of temper taught Polly caution. Puzzled, she wondered if Arabella was already bored with her, for frequently she departed to afternoon tea parties, leaving Polly to her own resources.

This was no hardship, for a friendship with Lucy Carmichael had developed and taking Oliver, who seemed a lonely little boy, the three would escape to the beckoning shore where cool breezes ruffled hair unhampered by bonnets and legs daringly bereft of stockings.

It was on a hot June day that as they sat watching schooners riding the waves Lucy cried impulsively, "Let's go for a dip."

"In the sea, you mean?"

"Where else, idiot? I've no doubt Oliver would love it."

Polly looked at the boy quickly. He had been dispirited for days by the thought of leaving his home for a new, unknown school, and a surge of sympathy swept over her. His broadcloth coat and breeches looked hot and uncomfortable and she immediately agreed with Lucy's suggestion.

"Off with your shirt then, but you'd better wear your breeches. We must remember to dry them thoroughly before returning home."

The boy grinned and laughing they all ran into the cool, shallow water. None could disturb them, for this particular spot was sheltered by a jutting rock and with gay abandon they splashed in the cool, refreshing ocean. Oliver showered the girls with spray and their shrieks delighted him until suddenly the sound of an explosion silenced them all. It came again and yet again and the child looked bewildered, whispering nervously "What is it?"

Together they took his hands, leading him on to the sand but their eyes met in perplexity.

"Sit in the sun and dry your breeches," Polly said, rubbing his back with her shawl. "There must be an explanation, don't be alarmed."

"I think it's probably gunners practising cannon in the Sound," Lucy comforted.

"How very astute of you, Miss Carmichael," came a

soft, unexpected voice, and quickly the three soaking figures spun round.

Smiling affably, his hat beneath his arm, shirt open at the throat, stood Richard Meredith. The sun an aura about his lofty head, his grey eyes flickered over them and Polly was acutely aware of her thin muslin dress clinging wetly to the contours of her body. That many women had purposely practised such a fashion but a few years ago was not unknown to her, but the city of Bath as a whole had frowned on such outrageous behaviour and never could she imagine doing such a wanton thing herself.

Lucy was obviously unconcerned, for with an engaging wink, she passed the humiliated Polly her shawl, and hugging it round her the defensive girl spoke to the smiling man.

"You always seem to find me in the most compromising situations, but it was so hot – "

"My dear Miss Fielding, I entirely agree. Far from blaming you I condone such a sensible idea and feel inclined to take a dip myself. Won't you all join me?"

"Oh, yes!" Oliver sprang forward eagerly. "Yes, please, sir. If it wasn't for the cannon we'd still be bathing. It *was* cannon I think, sir?"

"Quite right, Oliver."

Meredith was pulling the soft silk shirt over his head and Polly watched the muscles rippling on his golden skin. Obviously he was used to being exposed to the sun. "The guns are marking a solemn event, prompting forgotten loyalty. Our most sovereign lord, King George IV, is dead."

There was a biting note in the comment and Polly looked quickly into his face.

"An idle King and a tiresome one; England will not regret his passing."

"But the new King has no legitimate issue, and his wife is not young. How do you think we'll fare now?" asked Lucy.

"It depends on the Royal brothers and a fine race there'll be to produce a respectable heir. But why waste time on such problems, the day is warm and the sea too inviting."

Once in the water Polly was surprised to find Lucy striking out with long, powerful strokes, but she herself sat blissfully in the shallows watching the tall, handsome man encouraging Oliver to swim. That Arabella had once called him taciturn was beyond understanding; no man could be kinder to a small, nervous boy.

Her sole experience of young men, apart from domestic staff at school, was one effeminate music teacher, whose insufferably boring opinions and smell of stale wine, sickened her. She knew now, meeting a real man for the very first time, how much she had missed.

The cannons had ceased and Polly thought idly of the dead King, remembering a brief sight of him when he once passed through Bath years ago. The schoolgirls lined the route to the City and vividly she recalled the grotesquely fat man who seemed to overflow his ornate carriage, looking petulant and lonely.

When the bathing was over, Meredith took two large towels from the saddlebag of the gelding. He flung one to Lucy before briskly rubbing the boy until his skin glowed. Polly was then wrapped in the softness of the large towel and he patted her gently with his warm, brown hands, while over his shoulder Lucy grinned knowingly.

She felt no embarrassment as he rubbed her short,

red curls against his chest and a feeling of such rapture filled her that she trembled uncontrollably. He lifted her chin and looked into her eyes with a long, intent look.

"So green, so like the sea," he murmured only for her ears. "You should have been a mermaid, Polly."

He let her go abruptly and with disappointment she saw him turn, raising an arm in farewell.

Oliver was capering gleefully about but Polly stood silent, reluctant to show her rapturous face to the other girl.

"Sit down, for heaven's sake, and don't look so guilty," she was told. "The afternoon was to your liking, I'm sure."

"Of course it was, nothing so exciting has happened to me before. But I can't help feeling Arabella should have been present, she's been so touchy and depressed lately."

"Oh, stuff, it's probably love pangs that ail her, and can you honestly imagine Arabella frolicing so unseemly?" Lucy laughed.

"I suppose not, such a spree would be hardly fitting for Sir Richard's future wife."

"I doubt very much that gentleman is considering marriage at the moment. In spite of Arabella's aspirations, she's inclined to daydream, you know."

Polly called Oliver and as they set off together she tried to stem the feeling of elation Lucy's words had brought. Naturally, there had been no harm in the afternoon's pleasure but Arabella's face set with disapproval would flash before her eyes.

"It might be unwise to mention the episode; keep it to yourself," Lucy advised "and warn Oliver too."

Polly agreed and weaving a small conspiracy with the boy found him sharing their secret gleefully, as all children will.

None of them realised that high on the clifftop a lone rider viewed their departure from the shore, annoyance on his face as he turned his horse towards Stoke House.

Three

As he rode towards Budleigh steadily, for the air was too hot for his gelding, Richard Meredith brooded. The afternoon's revelry, innocent enough and correct in the presence of Lucy Carmichael had, nevertheless, distracted him. The sight of a shining-eyed elfin face alight with laughter haunted him to perplexity and he felt slightly irritated at his obsession with such a skimpy little creature. And yet, a few short hours in her company convinced him no other girl in the county had such a dainty charm, such riotous curls, or such enthusiasm for living.

He thought of Arabella Hamilton, prettily acceptable, waiting like a plump peach ready for the picking. With a figure suitably proportioned to provide him with heirs, with refinement and availability, she was, of course, the obvious choice for a man of thirty, prepared to settle down. Aunt Regina had persistently urged he take a wife and instil new blood into the Manor. Too long, she declared, the peaceful atmosphere had sheltered them both indolently, too long the house been void of music and laughter except for the annual masquerade where matrons' watchful eyes, with studied indifference, acknowledged his bows to their charges.

Love of the Manor and the land took priority over his bloodstock, but little else in life interested him. There was no living creature as faithful as his dog or the beautiful, glossy beasts he reared, and a reticence stemming from his lonely childhood erroneously labelled him laconic. He liked Devon folk, the farmers and their families, liked the Carmichaels and Hamiltons enough, but an inborn shyness kept him apart and the unconscious aloofness was unwittingly attributed to his position as Lord of the Manor.

He felt at ease with Arabella, who had the gift of serenity. She would not disrupt his house or his way of life, but quietly produce children in her placid way, and if respect and affection dwelt on both sides in a marriage, so much the better. He had been prepared apathetically to marry Arabella until she brought into his life without warning this other.

The diminutive Polly Fielding, with her quick little feet, was scampering into his heart and stirring emotions long since denied. Now the time had come to discuss his shifting interest with Aunt Regina, and riding through the trees towards his home, he stopped as the Manor came into view.

The beauty of it never failed to satisfy him, with turrets towering upwards in stark simplicity and mullioned windows facing the channel. Many said it stood like a fortress, stout and impregnable, but to Richard its very solidity acclaimed the strength of England. No doubt a wife would wish to pretty it up and change the sombre furnishings, but the tattered banners and tapestries of a bygone age must stay.

He looked up now, to see his aunt stretched comfortably on a couch by a first-floor window, and raised his hand in recognition. In spite of her peculiarities his love for her never faltered. She had

replaced the mother he never knew. His father had
spent a great deal of time in London frequenting the
then outrageous Prince of Wales set, and his
scandalous behaviour resounded through the county.
When he did periodically return to the Manor the local
population stabled their beasts and locked up their
daughters until the disreputable rake once more
departed.

Richard still remembered his early days, lonely and
lost in the great house, left to the care of local servants
and terrorised by the parson. But when Aunt Regina
returned to the district she attended to his education
and showered him with the love and compassion her
own childless state allowed. He ignored her eccentric
way of riding like a whirlwind, her painted face and
powdered hair and revealing clothes that scandalised
the neighbourhood. For the first time in his life there
was someone to love, and although on occasions she
and his father quarrelled savagely, raising the rafters
with furious oaths, they failed to disturb him. That
folk stayed away from two such violent people was no
trial to Regina. She had always preferred animals to
humans, and when her brother was killed by riding
drunkenly over the cliff one moonless night, she
showed little grief or dismay.

Twelve at the time, Richard was comfortably
absent at school but he inherited the title and returned
home for holidays with a new happiness. The
terrifying presence of his father gone, a close
relationship developed between himself and Regina
and they vowed to devote their lives to the land. It took
years to repair the neglect of his father, and Richard's
young manhood was dedicated to this and the stud he
founded.

The beautiful foals he reared were known and

revered and a pleasant undemanding life was enjoyed. But lately this contentment had been marred. Regina had contracted the dreaded dropsy and such painful swellings had developed to make her almost immobile. No longer could she enjoy riding or striding about the stables, but her brusque manner and tart tongue forbade sympathy, and her pride made no complaints.

As he climbed the stairs to her bedchamber, Richard was prepared for the heat that met him. A huge fire roared in the grate and the heavy scent of perfume was overpowering. Lady Regina reclined languidly, a pink shawl over her swollen legs and two great dogs lolled by her side, half dazed by the heat. She stretched out her arms towards him.

"It seems an abominable time since you left, my boy. Has Duchie foaled yet?"

He shook his head and bent to kiss the plump face smothered with white powder, while the clown's mouth smiled at him.

"God in heaven, it's stifling in here, Aunt. Allow me to open the window."

"Just a little, then. Take the dogs on to the balcony."

He obeyed her and fidgeted with the long silk drapes until her eyes scanned his face shrewdly.

"I've a fancy there's something afoot, my dear Richard."

He turned and laughed ruefully. "Nothing escapes you, I'll warrant, but changes to shock you might come about."

"Changes! Good God, boy, are you out of your mind?"

"Perhaps I am, or at least bewitched. My marriage, I feel, would not distress you, though?"

Her mouth fell open and with difficulty she spoke. "Distress me? Have I not continually urged the event for the past five years? So you've come to your senses at last. I'd like to hear what your tongue hangs out to tell, who is the gel?"

"One you've yet to meet. She's new to the county and quite delightful. I must confess to being greatly attracted."

The woman shifted uneasily on the couch and Richard came towards her.

"No facetious remarks, please Aunt, or jumping to immediate conclusions. I know little enough of her at present, neither am I aware of her feelings."

"I am unlikely to joke on a situation which you view with such seriousness, but the thought of a new face intrigues me. I must say I have never found the smug little pigeons of this town entrancing, although you seemed to favour the Hamilton wench."

"Arabella's still worth considering but you've shown her little favour."

"Don't fool with me, boy. If you wanted the gel you'd wed her even without my approval."

He grinned at her affectionately and she patted his hand.

"Speak up then, God forbid you'd be bashful with me!"

"Oddly enough, she resides at Stoke House and was brought from Bath as companion to Arabella. Her name is Polly Fielding."

"Polly? What sort of a name is that, for heaven's sake?"

"A diminutive of Mary, I believe, and there are other surprising things about her. She's full of *joie de vivre* and is tiny as a doll, with no great claim to beauty except for extraordinary eyes and hair like fire. If she'll accept me, Aunt Regina, I can think of no greater heaven."

For a moment the room was still as the woman looked into the face of her nephew. The wistful look it bore had been absent since childhood.

"I hope to understand, my boy, and trust infatuation has not blinded you; she sounds very young. Will she be a good breeder?"

"I feel that no longer has great importance, and a grand lady she'll never be. Her childish looks are deceptive, however, for life, I fear, has been harsh. She has no stylish name, no fine background, but I believe her capable enough to achieve success where other spoilt females might fail. She has dignity, Aunt Regina, and I love her."

"How many times have you and she met?"

"Too few, but I mean to rectify that. All I need is your approval."

"Tch! I've no doubt you'll do as you please whatever I say."

She saw the stubborn set of his mouth and was troubled. She knew him well enough to realise his love was not given lightly and yet how little, it seemed, was his knowledge of this girl. She frowned in concentration and then spoke quietly.

"I trust she will attend the masque, Richard, with all our guests in domino I shall find amusement picking her out of the crowd. It will take but a second to discover if she's worthy of you."

"But, by heaven, that means I must wait a month!"

"Just enough to stabilise your emotions, my boy, a very sensible suggestion, if I may say so."

Richard left the room and went down to his supper. Too many lonely meals had been taken in this great hall furnished with superb accoutrements, the handsome windows looking out to sea. He thought of minstrels playing in the gallery, of laughter and dancing beneath the sombre portraits, of rustling silk and fans and perfume, and he thought of fairy-like feet tripping in time to the music while a cluster of red curls rested on his shoulder. A girl who had never known love, strong and courageous and daintily beautiful, and he desired her above all other women. Together, children for St Mary's Manor would be created. Boys with red hair to ride his thoroughbreds and girls with green eyes to swing in his arms, every one born out of love.

The storm that greeted Polly when she appeared for supper was quite unpredicted, for she and Oliver had been successful in entering the house unobserved.

Her damp gown was changed but she refused to wash away the slightly salty feel of her body. She brushed her hair briskly, however, and donned new velvet slippers to match the brown ribbons on her sleeves before peeping into another room. Help was frequently needed with Arabella's toilet but finding the room vacant she ran down the stairs for fear of being late. John Hamilton was absent but Hugo and Arabella were already seated as Polly entered the dining-room, beaming brightly. As neither spoke she looked uncertainly from one to the other then suddenly recalling the cannons of the afternoon she spoke seriously.

"What sad news of the King; is that why you're both so solemn?"

"News? If such behaviour is considered news, you've extremely bad taste, Polly. Our neighbours would be scandalised." Arabella snapped.

"But everyone expected him to die soon – "

"What in heaven's name are you talking about?"

"The King's death, of course. We were on the beach and the cannons – "

Hugo gave a derisive snort. "Oh, we know where you were well enough, by God!"

Flushing, Polly turned to Arabella but the dark eyes surveyed her coldly.

"It is most unseemly to cavort in your underwear for all the world to see. Lucy Carmichael may be as unconventional as she pleases, her reputation rests on her wealth, but I simply cannot have my small brother exhibited to such behaviour. I trust Hugo was the sole spectator."

The temper that was prone to rise quickly in Polly rushed to the surface as she faced Hugo.

"You! How dare you spy on me, sir. A perfectly innocent afternoon was spent and neither Lucy nor I removed our clothing. We found pleasure in bathing in the cool water; am I to be blamed for that?"

"Keep your voice down, girl. Remember the occupants of this house are not without manners."

Polly fought to control her tears of rage. "Perhaps, but none were inherited by you, sir."

Hugo laughed. "I treat a lady with the respect she deserves, but you, miss, are no lady. I trust the fellow you sported with this afternoon is aware of that."

The colour faded from Polly's face and she glanced at Arabella uncertainly. Before an exchange could be made, however, John Hamilton entered with Aunt Sophia.

"Supper ready? There's no need to delay in respect for the deceased, life was perhaps impalatable under fatuous George but how we'll fare with William is a vexed question."

Without comment they started their meal, but a

discerning man, the father looked from daughter to son.

"Is something amiss? Come along, I'm not fool enough to be insensitive to atmosphere."

Arabella looked distantly out of the window but Hugo glanced across the table and a question was barked at him. "Well, Hugo?"

"Nothing to disturb you at all, Papa, merely an indiscretion on the part of Miss Fielding."

"Indiscretion? What the devil do you mean, sir?"

Polly looked up quickly, and spoke in a firm voice. "I'm afraid I foolishly took Oliver bathing in the sea, Mr Hamilton."

"Good heavens, is that all? There's no need to make a pother of so little a jaunt. Probably do the boy good, he needs some entertainment. We all agree on that, don't we, my dear?"

He spoke directly to Arabella and reluctantly she nodded.

Apprehensively, Polly waited for her further sins to be disclosed. Bathing with Lucy and Oliver was apparently acceptable but in the presence of a fully grown man, who knew what orgies might result? She felt a ripple of amusement at the absurdity of it all and Arabella's intolerance surprised her. Was she so dubious of Sir Richard's intentions in spite of her earlier innuendoes.

The streak of malevolence in Hugo she distrusted, but to her surprise neither he nor his sister made mention of Meredith in their father's presence. She felt, however, an apology from herself was necessary and spoke impulsively. "I'm so sorry you must think me the most inconsiderate creature. I realise I've behaved with imprudence – "

"Yes," Arabella nodded with a mollified

expression. "But kindly refrain from discussing it further. I do wish – "

An interruption came from the most unexpected quarter. Old Sophia, who for the most of the meal had behaved with restraint, suddenly gave an incredulous snort and pointed her knife at Polly. "Caroline Mary, that's who you are," she exclaimed loudly. "Your mother never recovered, poor thing, but mercifully went to her grave. It was a shocking thing, a shocking thing – so long ago.'"

Her voice trailed away and with a vague uncertain look, she peered at the head of the table where her brother sat.

"Be silent, Sophia," he said, not unkindly, "your ramblings are an embarrassment. I think you should rest now and Jane shall bring wine to your bed."

He rang for the maid and, puzzled, Polly watched him assist the frail figure to the door.

"Poor Sophia," he remarked, returning to the table. "Her hallucinations are quite a trial at times, you must forgive her, Polly my dear."

"But what a peculiar thing to say. Why did she call me Caroline Mary?"

"It is difficult to say, her memory plays strange tricks."

"Many years ago my aunt took a bad fall from her horse," Arabella explained. "She's been quite addled ever since."

"How dreadful, poor Miss Hamilton."

"It was a tragedy in many ways," John Hamilton took up the story. "She was to be married to a handsome young buck but the fellow ditched her unceremoniously after the accident."

"One couldn't really blame him, Papa, after all who would want a feeble-minded wife?"

Polly felt a sudden sympathy for the odd Sophia, whom she had frequently noticed in a garden gazebo facing out to sea. On occasion she had stopped beside her but found difficulty in conversing with one oblivious of her surroundings and strange unknown faces.

The memory of laughter and frolic in the ocean kept sleep at bay and in her oppressively warm room Polly recalled a husky male voice. She still felt the warmth of his hands when calling her a mermaid and she trembled with the joy of it.

No breath of air filtered through the open casement and she leaned out to see candlelight flickering through the wide open windows below. The sound of voices clearly rose, Hugo's sharp and slightly staccato, Mr Hamilton's calm and mellow and Arabella's curiously articulate.

The turn of the tide foretold the passing of midnight and something must be seriously afoot for a family conference at this hour. Listening intently Polly was astonished to hear her own name on Hamilton's lips.

"Although attaching little importance to this afternoon's affair in Polly's hearing, I really felt most disturbed by it. The girl was entrusted to your care, Arabella, but it seems your interests lie elsewhere."

"Such accusations are unfair, Papa. Bringing Polly to Stoke House was your suggestion and I am not her keeper. I simply refuse to let the wind play havoc with my looks for her entertainment and with Lucy so compatible what could be better?"

"Naturally, the Carmichael girl is beyond reproach, but I trust Meredith has no interest in the girl."

"Certainly not, Papa. He would not fail to be disgusted by such indelicate behaviour, I'm sure."

"You hope he was disgusted, by Gad," came

Hugo's derisive reply. "But don't make the mistake of believing Meredith's your sole prerogative. Polly Fielding's a dashed attractive wench. She could easily have a fellow with those eyes."

"What nonsense, Polly has no interest in men, certainly not Sir Richard. They have only met once."

"You think not? There are things your eyes never notice, Arabella. I'd advise you to snatch at the bait before your marriage plans go awry."

"I find you despicable, Hugo, with no sisterly loyalty to me."

There was a short silence, then the father's voice spoke soothingly. "Come, come. Kindly refrain from quarrelling and I'll beg you to guard your tongue, my boy. Your sister's attractions compare with any in the county and I have no fear for her future. But, we are not here to discuss Arabella's marital hopes, simply the fate of Miss Fielding."

"Oh, Papa. Are you about to reveal the intriguing mystery?"

"Not yet, my dear. It will be none the less sweet for the keeping, and a few more months will see my plans satisfactorily completed. I must stress, however, the importance of your co-operation, both of you showed discourtesy at supper and only Sophia's intervention prevented open conflict."

There was a pause and she heard the clink of glasses before he spoke again. "Tell me, boy. Do you find the girl pleasing?"

Hugo's explosive laughter infuriated Polly but she waited for his reply.

"Oh, she's fetching enough, an impertinent baggage and her temper needs curbing."

A window was closed and the voices below grew gradually fainter. The candles flickered out one by one

and all was dark and still. Polly turned from the
window towards her bed, collapsing on it in rage and
astonishment. That she was the object of their
discussion appeared surprising enough but she found
the mysterious undercurrent frightening. John
Hamilton's anxiety for her well-being seemed
disproportionate, for how could her presence disrupt
the course of their lives?

An uncomfortable feeling that Arabella had been
ordered to deliberately cultivate her for some devious
reason was shocking. Had the kindness and sympathy
she understood as genuine affection been merely a
charade to lure her into this house? If that was so, then
Arabella was as shallow as her hateful brother and the
kind benevolence of their father but a farce.

She recalled the strange words 'a few more months
will see my plans satisfactorily settled'. To what plans
was John Hamilton alluding? Did he possess some
secret knowledge of importance concerning her own
life?

A lump rose in Polly's throat. She had never felt so
cheated or humiliated in her life and her new-found
confidence was rapidly fading. How could she ever
hope to aspire to their world for all her pretences of
grandeur?

Gradually she grew calmer and as the angry tears
on her cheeks dried, the urge to gather her belongings
and rush headlong from the house subsided. Instead,
there rose a fierce determination to probe the puzzling
mystery. It was clear that both Hugo and Arabella
were as ignorant as she was of their father's tactics and
gradually a feeling of elation crept over her. She saw
no reason for objecting to the deferential behaviour
John Hamilton bid them adopt. She would accept
their homage calmly, revelling in their hypocrisy, but

no longer need she humble herself to Arabella or avoid the attentions of Hugo. Indeed, a little flirtatious caprice with that arrogant young man might be pleasing and perhaps deflate his ego.

As she fell asleep the smile of anticipation playing about Polly's lips turned to wistfulness as Richard Meredith's face flashed before her eyes. Arabella's confidence of one day reigning as mistress of St Mary's Manor was obviously still undaunted.

Four

The change of attitude towards Polly commenced almost at once but refusing to be impressed, she treated the Hamiltons' advances with her usual amiability.

When Hugo suggested she try her skill at riding her eyes flashed upwards but were quickly veiled. He was obviously aware of her dislike and a sudden capitulation might arouse suspicions.

In spite of this, however, the chance to learn control and understanding of a mount was advantageous, and meekly she assented.

Hugo seemed well pleased. "The cob is quite docile and should suit you nicely. I think this afternoon as good a time as any to start your lessons."

She found the saddle comfortable and Arabella obligingly provided a hastily adjusted blue habit. Her fear conquered, Polly sat proudly on the gentle Minnie as they trotted over the cliff top.

Hugo's eyes were full of appraisal. "You've a good seat and plenty of spirit, I'll swear you'd not complain if you took a toss."

"I've no intention of doing such an undignified thing," she answered tartly, tempted to tell him she had sat astride the most admired gelding in the county. But caution forbade it and Hugo, at his most charming, kept her trotting while relaying quips of scandalous gossip until laughter bubbled naturally from her lips.

After a while, resting under a tree, he looked at her with thoughtful eyes.

"There've been occasions when I've treated you with little respect. You'll not hold it against me, Polly?"

"If that's an apology I'll accept it," she answered lightly, but the words overheard lately were fresh in her mind and she regarded him coolly, drawing instinctively away as he raised her gloved hand to his lips, murmuring, "What a dashed attractive girl you are, Polly, with more spirit than any other I've met. I fancy you're ready now for a gallop."

With mischievous intent he flicked Minnie's rump with his whip and Polly clung to the reins, swaying dangerously in the saddle. Although vexed at his deliberate attempt to unseat her, the fright soon passed, for Minnie was lazy and quickly reverted to her usual steady trot.

Riding ahead while allowing her anger to cool, Polly found a new path almost invisible, thickly overgrown. Close by, a high wall was seen, and a pair of wrought-iron gates corroded by the years were standing slightly ajar. All was eerie and desolate, and pulling Minnie to a halt she peered through the gates into dense undergrowth. The outline of a house could be seen, with tall chimneys towering above the trees. Slipping to the ground, she passed through the gates before Hugo's impatient voice halted her.

"Come back, there's nothing to interest you here."

"You think not?" she answered, advancing further along the path. "My goodness, what a very large house, empty, I believe, and so silent and creepy."

"It's nothing but a filthy ruin destroyed by fire years ago. Said to be haunted, too, and avoided by sensible folk."

"Tell me about it."

She pushed aside the scrub to see vacant windows and the hollow shell of the house. "Is the ghost the former owner?"

"Very likely, but fire has scotched all the rumours. Now let me see you mount the cob."

To her satisfaction she achieved this feat without his aid and soon they returned to Stoke House.

As they rode up the drive, they saw that people were gathered on the terrace and a voice instantly recognisable brought a flush to Polly's cheeks. Richard Meredith rose from the seat beside Arabella and the faint smile so well remembered set her heart racing.

He came down the steps to offer her his arm and he glanced down at the red head scarcely reaching his shoulder. A wave of tenderness for this dainty little figure, which a puff of wind might blow away shot through him as her mermaid's eyes smiled into his.

"Arabella tells me you've been riding," he said with interest.

"Yes, indeed, at least I tried. I jogged along in the most ungainly manner and of course, there were some precarious moments."

"But Minnie's such a gentle creature," Arabella cried with amusement. "A baby could handle her, I'm sure."

Her face flushed, the dark eyes glowing, and looking extremely elegant in a pink afternoon gown, she was almost beautiful. Polly heard slight resentment in the voice and realised her own intrusion had disturbed a tête-à-tête. It must be obvious to all the world that Arabella was in love, and none could be better suited than she for a man in Sir Richard's position. Polly felt an intense longing to be like Arabella, cool, gracious and becoming, and only the flicker of interest in the grey eyes of the man by her side dispelled her own gloom.

"You have spread your wings on a docile beast," he said, "but only a firm hand and complete assurance is necessary with the friskiest mount."

"Well, I had no fear of Minnie", was her laughing reply, "although I do believe Hugo was impressed when a gallop failed to throw me."

"Perhaps soon I might have the pleasure of lending you a mare. I own a charming little filly, quite an angel in the most inexperienced hands."

Frowning, Arabella interrupted quickly. "Oh, but Hugo would be devastated at another's interference. He is quite determined to put Polly through her paces unaided. Apart from that, your lovely mounts must be too precious to entrust to an amateur."

"If Miss Fielding has been in the saddle all afternoon I consider her no longer an amateur."

"Oh, but I am, and yet I've never felt so confident." Polly boldly flashed a wicked smile at Arabella, who stiffened visibly while answering with a touch of acidity. "It is kind of you, Richard, to offer your help, and perhaps one day Polly will feel ready to accept your offer. But not at the moment, if you please."

He looked from one girl to the other, then nodded deferentially. "As you wish, of course."

As he departed, Polly sat down in the vacant chair and helped herself to a cup of tea. In spite of an outward calm her stomach fluttered with nerves and annoyance at Arabella's interference and yet she hesitated at provoking unpleasantness. She glanced furtively over her cup at the other girl, knowing with what difficulty Arabella's feelings were controlled.

Carefully choosing her words she spoke. "What a very kind man Sir Richard is."

"Very kind and also impulsive. I think perhaps you were a little forward with him, Polly. The offer to assist your riding was spurred only by generosity, you know. He understands your position and is anxious to help me transform you."

"Transform me?"

"Into a lady, my dear. But appearing over-familiar with the opposite sex is certainly no recommendation."

Her colour rising, it cost Polly an effort to speak calmly. "I appreciate your concern for me, Arabella, and I hope I'll never disgrace you. But sometimes I wonder what will happen to me when you leave Stoke House to wed. Is the possibility of marriage with Sir Richard true?"

Arabella gave a coy little laugh. "Perhaps." She paused and there were tears on her lashes. "I love him quite dreadfully, Polly – have done so for years. I don't think I'd ever consider another."

Polly rose and put a sympathetic arm around her shoulders. There was a wistfulness about the girl that moved her and the cold manner lately displayed was forgotten. She saw only a young woman hopelessly in love, waiting with longing for the sound of magic words and a pathetic sight it was.

Upstairs in her room the exuberant spirits of the

afternoon died. She who earlier had been exhilarated at the sight of two handsome men admiring her felt deflated. Admittedly, Hugo's attentions were false and yet he seemed not displeased with her company, but what of Sir Richard? The offer of his experience to a small, insignificant girl, whose heart beat wildly every time his grey eyes smiled, appeared genuine enough. How did that same man feel about Arabella, the girl who longed to be his wife, whose love could scarcely be contained in the hopes set so high?

Hugo proved an efficient tutor and Polly came to welcome his company, for Lucy had travelled north for a spell and Oliver sent off to Sherborne. Arabella seemed moody, for Sir Richard was abroad. "Away to tiresome horse sales in Ireland," she declared peevishly.

Sometimes the eyes of her brother snapped dangerously, but Polly now felt capable of dealing with the amorous Hugo and flirted gaily with him on occasion, confident of escaping unscathed. She chafed a little at the plodding Minnie's gait and thought of a livelier mare once promised.

Life was good, however, for a nip now appeared in the autumn air and fresh winds from the sea tore into Polly's hair, tossing her curls to fury. Often she discarded her hat or lost it in a gallop. One day it blew seawards and as she halted to retrieve it, Hugo was before her and they jumped from their mounts together. As she slid to the ground he imprisoned her in his grasp and bent his glittering eyes to meet her own startled ones.

"Polly," he whispered thickly, "have you any idea how beautiful you look at this moment? You tempt me to evil, you minx."

She struggled furiously in his grip but he laughed at her efforts. "You've tortured me enough, don't you know that? I simply cannot endure it."

Guiltily she suddenly became still and he kissed her while running his expert hands over her body. The kiss, unlike earlier lighthearted exchanges, filled Polly with distaste and she twisted in his arms. She was no innocent where sex was concerned, too many girls at school were seduced by unknown males, but she had no intention of allowing Hugo Hamilton the pleasure of her submission, he would have to beat her senseless first.

He swore violently as she slipped from his grasp and at that moment a crack like a whip caught him full in the face. Bewildered, Polly saw Hugo sent sprawling while incessant blows were rained on his stupified face.

She could not speak but stood helplessly by as at last Richard Meredith picked up the dazed Hugo and flinging him across the saddle sent his horse smartly towards town with a resounding slap.

Turning to Polly, his voice was grim. "Another compromising situation, Miss Fielding?"

"I do wish you'd stop calling me Miss Fielding," she replied through trembling lips. She was near to tears and he turned away, enabling her to control them while bringing Minnie forward.

"A miserable mount, as unsuitable for you as your name is, my dear. But if you insist, Polly it shall be."

Fully recovered now, she looked diffidently at him. "It seems you came to my aid all the way from Ireland. I really don't know what I'd have done without you."

"Not a pleasant thought," he answered curtly. "I feel England must restrain me now for a spell, if only to protect a child who's constantly getting into catastrophies."

"Oh, Sir Richard."

She dropped her shameful head and he put his hands on her waist before lifting her on to the cob and kissed her gently and firmly on the mouth.

"Your lips were meant to be kissed, Polly my dear, and don't look so startled. I'm not a despoiler like Hugo, but that wasn't unpleasant, was it?"

She shook her head, laughter gurgling in her throat. "Oh, no, not unpleasant at all, but perfectly acceptable, Richard."

His name slipped out naturally without its preceding title and he made as if to speak. But the moment passed and they trotted away perfectly at ease together.

"Do you still go down to the beach at night?" he asked.

"Sometimes, but now the nights grow cold and dark it is not so inviting."

"I regret being absent for such long periods, it is unavoidable. You are treated well by the Hamiltons, I hope, and are happy?"

"Of course."

An urge rose to reveal her doubts and fears to this understanding man, but strong loyalty to the Hamiltons forbade it. Also since that overheard discussion there had been no cause for complaint. She was treated with extreme courtesy by Mr Hamilton and Arabella, and Hugo, until this disastrous morning, had behaved with the utmost discretion.

"How is young Oliver faring at school?" he asked with interest.

"A little homesick, I fear, and of course I miss him. Fortunately, Lucy is returning this week, I enjoy her company. I wish Arabella enjoyed riding."

"She has a good seat, you know, but being a true female objects to the wind causing havoc with her looks. Possibly, too, she is concentrating on her costume for the ball. It surprises me to find you, too, are not busily engaged in creating some concoction."

Her puzzled look caused him to frown.

"I refer to the masquerade at St Mary's Manor, our annual event, attended by the county on St Michaelmas night. I trust my invitation has been accepted."

Polly smiled without comment, her mind busy with this surprising news. Although not fully aware of the importance of the masque, snatches of conversation between Arabella and her friends were recalled. Lucy, too, when one day enthusing over the Manor's splendour had mentioned last year's splendid event. But Polly had not envisaged a yearly occasion and neither was she warned about preparing a suitable gown. Was it possible the Hamiltons meant to exclude her from their party? Hurt by Arabella's deception she decided to await Lucy's return before questioning their actions.

Watchful and disheartened she went down to supper where Hugo appeared with numerous bruises and a cut lip. A muttered explanation involving a pesky stable door was offered and while ignoring his imploring glance, Polly found satisfaction in watching the perspiration gather on his face.

Things of the day were freely discussed without mention of the ball, and keeping her own counsel Polly wondered if close contact with the Hamiltons was teaching her their wiles. The unsavoury incident of that afternoon was concealed as was her meeting with Sir Richard and to a casual observer nothing deceptive or surreptitious surrounded the little party.

During the following days Arabella seemed anxious to be free of Polly's company, for she encouraged her riding, declaring too soon the weather would break bringing cool breezes and treacherous mists.

If she had doubts about her own behaviour, Polly soon dismissed them, for it was perfectly obvious some conspiracy prevailed at Stoke House, where Potter could be glimpsed scuttling about trailing scraps of crimson silk. Happy to leave the house, she wandered to the stables, where the saddling of Minnie now mastered, she prepared to ride out. The sight of Hugo hovering near amused her. His treatment over the last few days had been contrite and her half-smile at him brought an eager approach.

"I feel an apology is called for," he muttered bashfully. "It was good of you to spare me Papa's anger."

"I'm no tittle-tattle and your lesson was undoubtedly painful. The bruises are fading I see."

He fingered his lip tenderly. "Meredith's fists are like iron and his temper as hot as hell. Have you told Arabella about your champion?"

"Of course not, you know perfectly well her disapproval of violence. If she knew there were fisticuffs over me – "

"Her favourite beau and her brother, no less!" Hugo grinned painfully. "I'd watch that situation, if I were you."

"Thank you for the hint, I will. Now if you'll excuse me, Hugo, I'm off to the Carmichaels'."

His face fell. "I'd hoped for a ride together. Does forgiveness not include trust?"

Flicking her crop at him she rode out of the yard and on to the damp green grass. The road to Lucy's home was pleasantly lined with trees turning to gold, and glancing about in appreciation she noticed the lane where ancient chimneys rising from a derelict house were once glimpsed.

Thoughtfully she took the narrow track towards the rusty gates and dismounting tied Minnie to a sturdy tree. Blackthorn and ferns, brown now but rioting together made advancement difficult, for if ever a pathway existed it was long since gone.

She scarcely knew which way to approach the house now beckoning with a melancholy sadness, but pushing through brambles and nettles, snagging her skirt and stinging her hands, the heavy front door was eventually reached. Partly open, as were the gates, it hung dangerously loose, blackened with fire, and damp walls sagging against unstable beams smelled of decay.

Polly stepped inside but the rotten boards crumbled and a bruised ankle warned against further advance. She lifted her eyes to the lofty stairs, which had a neglected beauty, but the intricate balustrades, twisted and broken, were now bereft of dignity.

Turning away towards the rear of the house an orchard was seen still bearing fruit. The apples looked so inviting she stopped to pick one and a rabbit hopping along the high wall set her gaily leaping through the long grass after its scut.

The force with which she tripped over a square slab of granite left her breathless, and rising she pushed the weeds aside to find revealed a small headstone. Smoothing the neglected tablet with her hands she stared with curiosity at the simple words engraved there.

Caroline Mary Wintringham
November 2, 1794 – October 14, 1812
It were better thus.

Gently Polly traced the name with her finger. A girl
lay buried here, much her own age, too young to be
abandoned in the shadow of this mournful house.
Why was it better so?

Memory recalled Miss Sophia Hamilton's voice,
sharp with accusation, not long ago.

"Caroline Mary," she had said. "That's who you
are!"

Soberly returning to the cob, Polly went on her way
but distinctly voices denying the person of Caroline
Mary were remembered and the coincidence of the
hidden headstone seemed unanswerable.

The Carmichaels' house, long and rambling, had
little beauty but the wealthy Devon farmer and his
plump, elderly wife were hospitable. Lucy, born late of
a second marriage, had brought much joy to her
parents. Tragically, her mother's son by a former
marriage had died, and so the girl, their only kin, was
loved with devotion. Had her nature been less pleasant
she would have been disgracefully spoiled, for her
every wish was granted and her numerous friends ever
welcome.

Polly was greeted with pleasure and the two girls
chatted effusively, Lucy anxious for recent gossip and
Polly eager to discuss the surprising masque.

"You see what an awkward position I am in; it's
quite impossible to mention the event at Stoke
House," she complained.

"But you must and Richard's wishes be made
plain," came the indignant reply.

"How can they be when Arabella has no idea we

accidentally met. Neither does she know he and Hugo scuffled over me," Polly answered, describing the recent episode.

Lucy turned her head away. "Hugo's reputation is not of the best, but, frankly, I feel folk exaggerate. Was he very offensive?"

Surprised, Polly looked quickly at her friend, realising with surprise that Lucy cared for Hugo, and guilt at her own careless behaviour made her falter. "I suppose he meant no harm and you know how touchy I am. Perhaps I should have kept it to myself."

The other girl, composed now, turned with a faint smile. "Nonsense, I appreciate your confidence, for I've never been taken seriously in my life I'm simply known as an eccentric with few female charms to tempt the fellows. However, like many an heiress, I'm not obliged to marry."

The touch of bitterness in her voice was not lost upon Polly, but wisely she kept silent until Lucy, never subdued for long, shrugged.

"Now," she said, "how shall we face your problem, my dear. I can't believe Arabella would knowingly deceive, but their plot to deny you pleasure is mystifying. Sir Richard's wishes will naturally end all that, though. If he insists you attend the ball, go you shall."

"It seems quite impossible, Lucy. Think what an uproar I'd cause arriving without an escort and I certainly have no suitable dress."

"Do stop meeting trouble halfway. An escort is no problem, you must be my guest and, fortunately, work is about to start on my own costume. The seamstress shall stitch both!"

Polly's apprehension fell away as upstairs in Lucy's boudoir a box of glowing silk was rifled. She worried about a suitable dress to disguise her short figure.

"You shall dress as a procelain shepherdess," Lucy enthused "with a neat little bonnet to cover that tell-tale hair. None will be any the wiser until the unmasking."

"Unmasking?"

"Everyone removes their mask at midnight and many a fellow finds his partner not the beauty he thought."

They laughed with pleasure, discussing their plans and Polly, infected by Lucy's vivacity, no longer felt the hurt of Arabella's deceit. The thought of spending an evening beneath the grand roof of St Mary's Manor intoxicated her and not until returning to Stoke House was the grave of Caroline Mary recalled. She had completely forgotten to mention it to Lucy.

In her room Arabella spread out the red silk dress and looked for her brother's approval.

"It should suit you well enough" he remarked with little interest, draping himself negligently over a chair. "I wish I were half as pleased with my own choice, somehow I don't feel committed to the devil."

"Your face fits the image perfectly, particularly when in your present mood," his sister laughed. "But do try to control that headdress, it's mighty inconvenient for flirting and I don't want complaints from my friends."

Moodily Hugo picked at a cushion. "I think it damned unfair that Polly should be denied the fun."

"Well, it cannot be helped. Papa impressed the importance of keeping her away, although why simply puzzles me."

"She'll learn about it soon enough after the event, the whole county talks of nothing else for days and

Lucy's tongue will prattle. Meredith's enquiries might
be dashed awkward, too."

"Papa has some reasonable explanation, I'm sure,
as for gossip after the event I fail to see that it
matters."

"Our host might be full of concern for little Polly."

"You do make the most odious remarks. Why ever
should Richard feel protective towards her. Have you
been stirring up mischief?"

He waved an airy hand as he left the room and
Arabella frowned thoughtfully. Her father's attitude
was indeed puzzling and such avid secrecy troubled
her. Polly must have heard rumours by now of the
topic on everyone's lips. She had shown no cuiriosity,
nor remarked on Potter's regular attendance. It all
seemed highly irregular.

Five

Polly thought the Hamiltons would never leave the
house and many times the little clock in her room
received an anxious glance. Standing in the shadow of
a curtain she at last watched the carriage roll away,
unable to see that Arabella's eyes swept her candlelit
window with relief.

In her masquerade she stood filled with misgivings
before the mirror. The pastel blue panniers and laced
bodice appeared absurdly youthful and the short skirt
revealing her legs in white silk stockings was positively
childish. That those beautifully shaped limbs might
cause a man's heart to flutter never occurred to her as

with hat and crook concealed under a long cloak she left the house and hurried to the crossroads where she and Lucy had arranged to meet. How fortunate it was that doting parents allowed her friend a small vehicle of her own and, according to plan, Polly climbed with haste into the waiting carriage.

"I'll never have the courage to unmask," she confessed as they bowled along. "The thought of Mr Hamilton's horrified face makes me shudder."

"We'll consider that later. At the moment think only of the pleasures to come, and young bucks fighting for your favours."

Polly grinned happily, appraising the tall Lucy, who looked transformed in a shimmering silver and green sari.

The drive to the Manor was lined with coaches, and music and laughter floated from the great house. The two girls, their masks firmly fixed, were immediately surrounded as they entered the hall by gentlemen in an assortment of comical costumes.

At once a gay cavalier swept Polly into the dance, while steps learned in former days carried her lightly over the floor. Partners there were aplenty, and quickly she became expert at dodging mischievous hands anxious to dislodge her mask. Intoxicated with happiness, laughing and flirting, she slipped from over-ardent caresses, yet her eager eyes behind their velvet shield never ceased searching for Richard Meredith. But that gentleman was not in evidence and his absence, now notable, was causing comment, particularly from sofas where elderly matrons showed their marked disapproval. Fans fluttered rapidly in speculation at their host's inattentive behaviour, and Polly wondered were he always so ill-mannered.

A fierce-looking devil in scarlet put an end to

contemplation by sweeping her away, the horns on his head in danger of dislodging her bonnet as he bent to whisper humorously, "Well done, dear Polly, a splendid disguise."

Instantly she stiffened but without missing a step. She might have guessed Hugo would have the effrontery to impersonate Satan and she answered pertly, "I feel your choice of costume very apt, Hugo."

"What would you say if I put the image to use and stirred up the devil's own trouble? You should be shaking in your little shoes, my dear."

Bravely determined not to show how near the truth he was, she smiled with extra brilliance and his hands tightened on hers.

"Don't worry, your secret is perfectly safe with me. One good turn deserves another is my motto, Polly, and I'm dashed pleased you came."

"Thank you. It was clever of you to recognise me so soon. I can't seem to penetrate anyone's disguise except Arabella's, of course. She looks quite delightful."

"I must say that Spanish gown is appropriate and most conspicuous."

"I only hope my own is less so. I'd be mortified if your father discovered me."

"Do you intend playing Cinderella and slipping away before midnight?"

"That is the general idea."

Hugo laughed as the cotillion ended and Polly quickly escaped his arms to slip behind a pillar, for Richard had at last entered the room. Contrarily she wished to hide, but soon he stood formidably close she could scarcely acknowledge his greeting.

"Are you by any chance trying to evade me?"

"Not exactly, sir, but perhaps disappointed at such

instant recognition."

"To me you are unmistakable, no other has your miniature grace. I trust you found enjoyment in the dancing, for surely there was no lack of partners?"

"Certainly not," she answered with impulsive reproof. "The evening is well gone, sir. How should I have fared awaiting your favours?"

"Ill, I do declare. I trust you'll forgive my neglect."

Polly blushed, her lips trembling between laughter and mortification.

"I am insolent, sir, it is I who should apologise."

"If you insist on self-denunciation I shall whip off that ridiculous hat you wear and quite possibly kiss you here and now."

He caught her hands and expertly swept her into the line of dancers. Faultlessly dressed in a blue velvet coat, the only person without domino, and the focus of so many eyes he danced his shepherdess across the floor. No other man could claim her, but tiring of the music at last they wandered into the dim, cool hall, where he bent to her ear.

"Dearest Polly, could you bear to forgo the music? I have an urge to show you my house."

Her spirits soaring with the pressure of his hand on her arm, she looked to the lofty staircase where battle-torn banners stirred proudly among the portraits.

"I would be honoured, for it seems the whole must indeed be beautiful."

"None more so. But perhaps I am biased. You shall be the judge."

He steered her through a wide archway to narrow steps hidden from prying eyes and climbing to upper floors, the splendour left Polly gasping. When they halted before a massive white door she looked at him uncertainly, aware how suddenly grave were his eyes when he spoke in a low voice.

"My aunt resides in these quarters and I fear she is far from well. It was my intention to cancel the ball but her stubborn pride forbade it. She did however request – no, command – I bring you to visit her my praises are enough to arouse her curiosity."

As he moved to open the door Polly put her hand on his arm. "I feel so dreadfully nervous."

"What nonsense, she's not a dragon, you know, but the kindest creature to those she loves. I am more than devoted to Aunt Regina, although such adulation would vex her considerably."

"She may not approve of me at all," she murmured as he opened the door, revealing a large room lit by many candles.

Polly's eyes flew instantly to the enormous bed, where propped against pillows lay a plump, pink-faced woman with coquettish patches and yellow hair too brilliant for nature's art.

"I've brought the visitor you wished to see," Richard smiled, ushering the girl forward. "Miss Polly Fielding, as dainty a shepherdess as any among your Meissen treasures."

A plump hand reached out.

"A charming little thing I do declare. You have no fear of a gross old woman, I trust? Come into the light, child, and let me see what lies behind that idiotic disguise."

Removing the mask and the whispy little hat, Polly approached the bed, as Regina heaved up her bulk, groping for a quizzing-glass. She raised it to scrutinise the young face for a full long minute, then sighing, waved a languid hand.

"Take her away, Richard, I find young things quite wearisome. Have I reared you to treat your guests with contempt, begone to your duties."

With brief dismissal she turned away and Richard led the tremulous Polly from the room.

"You must forgive her, the visit was perhaps ill timed, but you shall meet again in happier circumstances, for your mutual liking is important to me."

A quiver at his words dispelled the gloom of so discouraging a welcome and as the clock struck midnight, Polly adjusted her mask, Richard flicked it, smiling. "A little late for that, my dear, the hour of revelation is come. Hold tight to my arm, I see the ballroom is in darkness."

As they descended to the dim, breathless ballroom new lamps were being lit slowly, one by one, and when discarded dominos fell to the floor shrieks of laughter were heard mingling with gasps, some of delight, others of dismay.

Looking swiftly about the freshly lit room Polly returned Lucy's vigorous wave while her eyes sought Arabella. She saw Mr Hamilton chatting with several chaperons, unaware yet of her unexpected presence until one or two young people spied her and cried indignantly.

"Unmask, unmask, you rascally cheat!"

It seemed the whole company turned its eyes upon the one standing close to their host and when Richard teasingly whipped away both mask and hat she was full of apprehension.

Hamilton, turning to view the focus of all eyes, had little time to stare, for a commotion among his elderly companions immediately distracted him. They stood, a flutter of agitation, their quivering fans surprising the younger folk, and puzzled looks passed from them to the confused little shepherdess.

The barrage of eyes filled Polly with panic as Richard left her side to investigate such curious conduct, but whispers flying from mouth to mouth seemed to rise into a crescendo of sound and with racing heart she turned and fled into the chilly night.

Down towards the beach she sped, away from those accusing eyes, tearing her flower-trimmed dress as she scrambled in fright to the tranquil shore.

Crouching under the cliff her tears fell with abandon, tears of angry frustration at her own naivete. She saw only too well how scornfully those contemptuous women had rejected her. She was an unpaid servant forgetting her place. How dare she intrude in their chosen world, she a charity child? Even Lady Regina, in spite of Richard's excuses, regarded her with disfavour and her condemnation above all others provided the final humiliation.

So incensed was she that the gentle hands on her shoulders seemed but a dream until his warmth became reality.

"Richard," she whispered, "Richard?"

Her head was drawn tenderly to his chest. "Darling Polly, who else? Does any other know of your secret haven or consider you a mermaid?"

He wiped her face but his comfort evoked fresh tears and she sobbed.

"Did you see their scornful eyes, their haughty stares? I've always believed true ladies kept their feelings hidden, but even the lowest scullery maid would show better manners."

"It was unforgivable, I agree. Such behaviour by friends of long standing puzzles me, and even advanced age cannot excuse discourtesy. I beg you return to the house with me, where apologies shall be made."

She shrank away, shaking her head and he turned it
to meet his eyes. As the moon slid gracefully from a
cloud she saw his intent gaze and his mouth covered
her own quivering one with kisses.

"Dearest Polly, who cares for the whims of others,
my love will shield you for ever. I've loved you since
the day we met and no other can satisfy me now. Do
you doubt it when we have this — and this?"

He kissed her eyes and her hair, murmuring
endearments while she lay against his heart, soothed
and comforted. The sound of the sea was their serenade
and Richard laughed softly.

"I hardly expected to make a proposal with sand for
my knees and a shoulder damp with tears. But can
you forgive the lack of convention and hear an
impatient lover out? It will take but minutes, for my
heart beats must surely drown what words I utter. I
love you, my darling shepherdess, with such devotion,
and I'm asking you to be my wife."

Stunned, she sat, too full to speak, tremulous with
longing but savouring his lips that touched her
wherever possible. When at last she spoke, it was a
whisper. "Is it really possible for you to marry me?"

"Why not indeed?" He frowned, suddenly sober.
"Am I to understand you don't care for me?"

"Oh, no, I love you very dearly, but the thought of
St Mary's Manor frightens me a little, and there's also
Arabella."

"A fig for Arabella! There is nothing but friendship
between us and the Manor is not as forbidding as it
looks. It needs a fresh face, new ideas, and your own
sweet company. I fear I have been a neglectful squire
but the whole locality shall benefit from our union as
we raise our family among them."

"Oh, I hope so, for I've come to love the county with

all my heart." Her eyes suddenly searched his face. "But your Aunt Regina, Richard, I feel she may be displeased. How will the thought of a strange girl intruding, affect her? A girl with nothing for recommendation, not even a name of her own?"

"No name? Is Fielding so ignoble?"

"I suppose not, if it is truly mine. So many foundlings received assumed names and I fear one of them was me."

"You know nothing of your parentage?"

"Nothing." She shook her head. "Of course as I grew older my curiousity grew with me, but it never was satisfied."

"Well, one day we shall attend to that, sufficient at the moment is our love. Time is too precious and the night too beautiful for such trivial things."

They kissed and walked along the shore hand in hand, and with hurt and humiliation forgotten, Polly clung to her knight in ecstasy. Her new-found love brought a forbidden glimpse of Heaven and the sand she trod was a field of stars.

The atmosphere at breakfast next morning was sultry, but Polly, her head in the clouds, soared above such trivialities.

Her refusal to return to the Manor with Richard last night was accepted with understanding, and she sat quietly transfigured, waiting in Lucy's carriage. Only a loyalty to the Hamiltons prevented the disclosure of such stupendous news to her curious friend, who drove them back to Stoke House in silence.

Now, demure beneath John Hamilton's disapproving eye, she glanced at Arabella, tight-lipped and glowering, while waiting for the storm to break. When he spoke the man's voice was heavily

ponderous. "I trust you realise the mortification your
behaviour caused last night, Miss Fielding, and I fail
to recollect permitting your attendance at the ball."

"But, Mr Hamilton," Polly answered quietly. "I
did not falsely intrude. Sir Richard issued a personal
invitation to me."

Arabella icily intervened. "That seems very odd and
quite unacceptable. I suspect you learned of the event
through Lucy Carmichael and decided to savour its
pleasure yourself."

"Do you doubt my word, Arabella?"

Before a reply came Hugo said helpfully. "The
personal request might well be true, I've seen them
meet on occasion."

His sister's brows drew together ominously but
their father raised his hand.

"Quarelling cannot mend matters, Arabella, let the
affair rest there. But I would appreciate a few words
with you in my study, Polly, if you please."

The severity of his voice would, a few months ago,
have caused Polly some distress, but secure now in her
golden future, she was capable of facing the world and
its extremities. The moment for breaking her own
startling news was approaching and with anticipation
she awaited their reactions, regretful at hurting
Arabella, but determined not to weaken.

While awaiting her reprimand she watched the
pursed lips and frowning face before her with calm.

"You must forgive Arabella's accusations, she is
quite put out by your scandalous behaviour." His
voice was testy and plump fingers tapped his desk
irritably.

"But, Mr Hamilton, I still don't understand what
dreadful act I've committed, nor why I was purposely
prevented from attending the ball. The hostile

reception I received at the unmasking is, I feel, punishment enough. It was totally unexpected, but perhaps I am mistaken in believing you welcomed me to Stoke House as an equal. Would you prefer to see me residing in the servants' quarters?"

"Kindly refrain from impertinence, it is not your place to question my actions, neither, I hope, are you treated other than as a friend of my daughter. However, I am disappointed and greatly displeased at your clandestine behaviour and I fear Lucy Carmichael's influence does you no credit."

"Lucy has been a good friend, sir, the only true one I have, it seems."

He sighed. "It would grieve Arabella to hear such remarks, she is most disturbed by your conduct. In spite of that she holds you in high esteem, although time is needed to recover her pride and repair the damage of your thoughtless act. I have spent a few sleepless hours myself on your behalf, and feel it wise to send you away for a while."

Polly stared at him wide-eyed. "You mean I'm to leave Stoke House?"

"Merely a temporary arrangement. My sister needs a girl in her London home, a few months there would not come amiss."

She braced herself to face him without flinching. "I'm afraid such a plan is impossible, Mr Hamilton. you see I recently received a proposal and my fiancé would take the suggestion unkindly."

"A proposal girl! Kindly explain."

"It is all very simple. Last night Sir Richard Meredith asked for my hand in marriage. Needless to say, I accepted."

His eyes bulged with such amazement that amusement bubbled inside her as she murmured demurely. "I trust you are not displeased, sir."

"Displeased! Good God, I am quite overcome," he
spluttered. "Neither can I believe such a preposterous
tale is true. Sir Richard has nigh spoken for Arabella,
have you bewitched the fellow into a proposition?"

"I think not, sir, we are very much in love."

"Love! What does a chit like you know of love?
Secret assignations no doubt have turned sweet talk
into marriage vows. I'll not believe such nonsense,
until I hear it from the fellow's own lips. Please get
your cloak and accompany me to the Manor without
delay."

At his sharp voice Polly ran upstairs, eyes snapping
dangerously. To be suspected of fabrication was bad
enough, but the man, considering her beneath a
nobleman's glance, was due for a rude awakening.
With Richard beside her, firm and proud, there was
nothing to fear and a confrontation only pleasing.

As the carriage passed through the gates of St
Mary's, Polly kept a cool countenance although
inwardly tremulous. She looked with slight contempt
at her companion, who had fidgeted and fretted the
whole way from Stoke House, but the bustle and
activity about the grounds distracted her as men
cleared the debris of the ball.

A liveried footman aloof and impassive, met them
on the steps and Hamilton nodded in his usual polite
way.

"I would see your master, my good fellow. Advise
him John Hamilton awaits."

Giving a slight bow the other spoke calmly. "Your
errand is futile, sir. My master is not in residence."

"Come, come, his reluctance to appear is
understood, we all feel fatigued this morning. But the
matter is urgent, if he's abed, I'll wait."

Feeling slightly nervous, Polly stepped forward impulsively.

"Please tell Sir Richard Miss Fielding is here. I'm quite sure he'll not refuse me."

"Regretfully, miss, I must repeat myself. Sir Richard left the Manor at dawn complete with excessive baggage."

"Left? But to where? Kindly tell me his destination."

"The Master did not disclose it, miss, it is not my place to question my superiors."

Bewildered and frustrated she looked into Hamilton's face. The smug, self-confident look made her throw off his restraining hand as she turned once more to the servant.

"Lady Regina. Please take me at once to Lady Regina; she will understand. Tell her – "

"My lady requested no visitors, miss. I cannot disobey orders."

Perplexed by Richard's unexpected absence and distrustful of the man at her side, Polly re-entered the carriage helplessly. To his credit, Hamilton made no comment until a mile or so were passed, then he spoke not unkindly.

"I fear your good nature and youth have been exploited, my dear. But do not be disheartened, one learns by mistakes how to face disappointment. There will be other beaux no doubt; perhaps you might count Hugo among them."

If he thought to hearten her, how vain was that hope, and it cost an effort to keep stonily silent. Whatever remark she made would be misconstrued and she realised how sceptically her tale was acknowledged. Its authenticity, without Richard's support, was undeniably suspect and what excuse had she for his desertion?

Convinced that good cause lay behind his departure, nothing could shake her belief in his love and engrossed in thought she heard but the remains of a sentence.

" – you will fully understand why I wish to send you to my sister."

An alarming recollection of his earlier proposition found her facing him in dismay.

"New surroundings cannot but stimulate your wits," he was saying. "It will please you to hear I have no intention of recounting to Arabella this little episode, and I trust you'll forget such nonsense. Be a dear, good girl and you shall come home for Christmas. With great inconvenience I'll escort you to London myself. Kindly be ready to travel on the afternoon coach.

Sickened, Polly realised she had no choice. They were throwing her away like an unwanted vessel and only pride prevented her showing defeat as they left in the London-bound coach. The unperturbed face of John Hamilton brought reassurance as did his promise of Christmas, and there was simply no point in behaving irrationally when her stay in London would most certainly be brief. When Richard returned from his unexpected trip, her urgent letters awaiting would naturally bring him swiftly to her rescue and she dreamed of a triumphant return to the foolish and repentant Hamiltons.

A cool farewell from Arabella was disconcerting, but her dignity unimpaired, Polly accepted the gift of a pretty reticule and the promise of constant letters. When, after a few days, the first one arrived however, it was filled with reproving advice. Arabella trusted her dearest friend was well and enjoying her stay in a city so renowned, continuing:

"I do trust, dear Polly, you will take the advice of a more experienced friend and conduct yourself with greater decorum. The night of the masquerade revealed how very vulnerable you are and your behaviour with Sir Richard Meredith was quite unseemly. I must warn you that a mere kind gesture on his part might easily be misconstrued and I fear you know little of nobility or how they trifle with unsuspecting hearts."

Flushed and angry, Polly flung the letter aside. Six days had passed in the house of Mrs Frances Lloyd, a female counterpart of her brother, John Hamilton. She was obviously vexed at a tiresome wench unexpectedly thrust upon her and she greeted Polly with suspicion. Her London house, staffed with an army of superior servants, was smoothly and efficiently run and Polly soon found herself an unnecessary addition. The small errands executed were trivial and she quickly became bored, her only distraction the spacious garden. But the formal beds and neatly trimmed hedges had not the joy of a wild, breezy clifftop and she missed riding an amiable Minnie and the soothing sound of the sea. Although there was entertainment in viewing grand emporiums and fashionably dressed crowds, congestion, clattering traffic and the raucous cry of street vendors held little magic for her.

On the first evening she penned a long, entreating letter to Richard, but difficulty in finding a mail coach arose and anxious moments were spent seeking opportunities.

"If you have letters for posting, leave them with my maid," Mrs Lloyd graciously conceded, but Polly kept that particular one firmly in her pocket, perhaps wrongly distrusting the kind gesture.

Eventually the problem was solved by enclosing the letter in one to Lucy and on hearing it was duly delivered she became less apprehensive. His appearance on the doorstep was half expected but, as day after day went by, she fought a battle with desperation, longing to see his face, longing for the strength of his arms, wondering if perhaps, after all, such happiness had been only a dream.

Six

London was crowded, for many expected a coronation before the year's end, and if rumours of postponement abounded, everyone ignored such doleful news. None believed the empty government coffers were incapable of providing a celebration, and the pomp and pageantry of a crowning was eagerly anticipated..

But Parliament kept from a riotous public how drastically their late King had beggared them, and were wary of fixing a definite date for such an extravagant event.

The Londoners' disappointment was shared by Polly and for all the bustling crowds and over-stocked shops, little excitement prevailed. An occasional procession, the King's Guards, or a glimpse of an elaborate carriage was all she ever saw of royalty and such an over-rated place as the capital provoked her.

Many spare hours were spent in reading, for Mrs Lloyd graciously offered her use of the library and here an abundance of writing-paper encouraged the penning of letters.

Lengthy epistles to Oliver, describing what few events she witnessed, were made, while others were blatantly fabricated simply for his amusement. From the boy's own sketchy notes, a loneliness akin to her own was sensed and the solitude abounding in a large school an experience she remembered. Politeness necessitated writing letters to Arabella as well.

Lucy, a born writer, sent lengthy descriptions of her travels. She also wrote of Devon, bringing to Polly the red hills, the sea and open heath, bringing also a vision of the burnt-out house with soft falling leaves quietly obscuring the grave of Caroline Mary. She felt a need to probe that faint, perplexing mystery and her own neglect of past lazy summer days was regretted.

October passed and with it Polly's eighteenth birthday, remembered by none. Now November brought treacherous fogs and a letter from Lucy Carmichael to break her heart.

"Dearest Polly," it ran. "You must forgive my tardiness, but on returning home from the north I had hoped to find you reinstated at Stoke House. I do trust to see you ere long, for much has happened during my absence, events that will astound, but not, I hope, distress you.

"Sir Richard is back at the Manor after an absence of weeks. He may have been to Ireland, of course, but it is rumoured London claimed him. Your last letter refrained from mentioning his name so I presume your paths did not cross, but London is a vast place and I understand he has many friends in the capital.

"Now, what I find most mystifying is how he regularly seeks Arabella's company. She is unusually reticent and as smug as a cat full of cream, but Sarah believes their engagement is imminent. Does it mean

Arabella has achieved her desire at last, or am I being presumptive? I've often felt an attraction between yourself and Sir Richard exists. If this is so there must be a reason for keeping me in ignorance, but always remember, dear Polly, I am your sincere friend ... "

The letter fell from Polly's shaking hands, the implication of Lucy's words beating in her head. Richard and Arabella to be married? How could that possibly be, when the love shared so passionately on a moonlit shore still haunted her. Sarah was a gossip, a muddle-headed goose adept at mixing fantasy with fact.

The thought of her own letters, so desperately sent to the Manor, filled her with fear. Surely he was aware of her plight or were the ominous words of Arabella true, he had trifled carelessly with so willing a victim.

Foresaken and alone, she fought the bitter tears. There had been many times when sunk in a slough of despair, her natural optimism had surfaced, providing resolute courage for battle. Never before had such heartbreak engulfed her but a firm determination to discover the truth set her, without hesitation, planning an escape from London.

She had realised from the beginning that making an enemy of Mrs Lloyd was foolish. Her unavoidable stay in this sumptuous house should be as pleasant as possible, and obedient and self-effacing, the meek manner deliberately adopted won her plenty of licence. The problem of money for the illicit journey did not trouble Polly unduly, she had never in her life owned any of her own and treated it with little importance. The only thing of value she possessed was a small gold locket, a gift from Arabella, and feeling no sentiment for it now, sold it for half a guinea. This would pay her coach fare to Winchester, and the sooner the better, for compulsion drove her relentlessly. Return to Devon she must, to discover for herself if Richard's conduct be true or false, and no longer was self-pity acceptable.

Choosing her moment carefully while the family dined with friends, Polly slipped unobserved from the house and was soon on the coach. After a long and tiring journey, hampered by lame horses, she alighted the following evening and set forth on her own tireless legs. Exhilaration replaced the depression as, wrapped in her protective cloak, she passed the milestones pointing south. Almost halfway there, how jauntily she stepped along! What matter if it took her weeks, she was journeying back to the sea, now in winter, grey and chill, but none the less, enchanting.

A belt of rain blew across the open plains and for days she walked in soaking clothes, resting at night in the odd hay barn, stealing milk and cheese from an untended dairy until the smell of salty air reached her nostrils and red cliffs appeared through variable mists. Daylight was fading and she was still some way from the Carmichael's farm where, relying on that family's spontaneous hospitality she hoped to be received without question, when confused by the mist and in total exhaustion, she sank by the shelter of a wall. There was strange, familiar comfort in this resting-place, and she slept until awoken by a pale winter sun. Ravenously hungry and chilled to the bone, she rubbed a little life into her frozen limbs while surveying her position, and with delighted surprise she found herself against the garden wall of the old burnt-out house. On the other side lay Caroline Mary Wintringham, and somehow it seemed oddly coincidental to find herself there.

With stiff legs she walked into the morning sun, not

heeding the sound of galloping hooves until they were almost upon her. The black horse reared alarmingly and his rider's angry voice barked.

"What the devil — "

Immediately aware of her sorry appearance, cloak torn, shoes in ribbons and an air of general dishevelment, Polly could not trust her voice as she looked up into the face that once had gazed on her with love. Giving her a swift glance he dismounted.

"What, may I ask, are you doing here in such a bedraggled condition?"

Heart sinking, she faltered unhappily, "Well, you see, I've walked from Winchester — "

"Good God, I don't believe it!"

Her anger rose at the remarks, overriding the hurt of his sour welcome, and although his eyes were in shadow, the lack of concern was apparent. There was no delight in this sudden encounter and how true it seemed were Lucy's suspicions of his dalliance with Arabella. She gritted her teeth in defiance. Never would their earlier relationship be recalled, she would die first, but neither would pity or contempt be accepted.

Proudly she lifted her head, the green eyes glittering. "I fail to see how my affairs concern you, sir, but kindly oblige by keeping my presence here a secret."

"Do you not intend returning to Stoke House then? I fear John Hamilton will be displeased at your disgraceful behaviour. May I ask? — "

"You may ask nothing, for I consider you quite untrustworthy. Neither shall I satisfy your impertinent curiosity; please allow me to pass, Sir Richard."

"That I cannot do, my dear."

Without warning he snatched her up and leapt on to the horse with Polly furiously beating at him in despair.

"If you take me to the Hamiltons I'll kill you!"

She clung to the saddle, knowing every ounce of strength was gone, only half aware the towers of St Mary's Manor loomed increasingly larger. But the firm arms of Richard brought a surge of happiness and in spite of their bitter encounter her heart remembered. Closing her eyes she drank in his nearness and somehow, the future mattered not at all. This moment to add to her memories was savoured lovingly.

Scrubbed and clean, her riotous curls once more shining, Polly sat in a green wrapper several sizes too large and faced Richard Meredith. When he spoke it was with cool courtesy as if conversing with a stranger.

"I see you are now presentable and have eaten well, I believe, but your improbable situation fills me with curiosity. Suppose you tell me what happened."

"I thank you for your hospitality, but cannot believe my welfare interests you, sir," she answered, her feelings under firm control.

"Once, long ago, I begged you not to call me sir," he answered, the bitterness in his voice filling her with wonder.

"Is that bond between us still remembered? I fancied it forgotten with my banishment to London. I waited so long for your coming." The words were out before she could control them and biting her lip with annoyance she waited.

He rose and faced the window. "The Hamiltons kept me informed of events. Were you so unhappy, then?"

"One cannot be happy when an unwilling prisoner."

He turned and coming forward, took her hands impulsively, but angrily, with stormy eyes, she snatched them away.

"You cannot fool me with your false concern; no longer am I stupid and naive."

"Naive perhaps, but never stupid. It would please me if you'd forget what has gone and words that were better unsaid."

Pain squeezed her heart as she whispered. "So it's quite true, you mean to marry Arabella?"

"News travels fast to London, I see. My harsh treatment is regretted, and without expecting forgiveness, I can only hope that one day your questions will be answered. Can you bring yourself to tell me why you so suddenly returned?"

Never should he have the satisfaction of knowing the true cause and shrugging lightly, she played for time.

"I've told you I was unhappy there and Lucy suggested – "

"Ah, the Carmichael girl, she's invited you to the farm?"

"Not exactly but she is kind and, while not intending to impose, I felt that for a while I might – could – " She paused confused and stammering.

"A pity you failed to check Lucy's movements. Her family are noted for travelling and at the moment are away on one of their jaunts."

Feeling helplessly lost and alone she fought to hide her dismay but when he spoke his voice was gentle.

"I feel you should rest now, I'll wager it's weeks since you slept without fear. A room is already prepared, sleep well, and ignore the gossip."

Aghast she gaped at him. "Here? But I cannot stay

here?"

"Why ever not, pray? As Stoke House is so obnoxious there seems little alternative. We cannot allow you to tramp the road like a gypsy."

The genuine concern in his eyes filled her with sudden confusion, but physically and mentally more weary than ever before in her young life, the thought of a comfortable bed was like a soothing drug, lulling stresses and problems into unimportance.

For twenty-four hours she slept and awoke half ashamed, but much refreshed. With surprise she noticed by the bed a neat pile of clothes for her convenience and after hasty ablutions, scrambled quickly into them. With what style the ecru lace trimmed a soft lilac gown! In slippers that amazingly fitted, she ran down the handsome staircase to find Richard waiting below. He waved away her thanks with a smile.

"Let me look at you. The gown's a trifle long, I fear, but otherwise my memory played no tricks."

Quickly she looked up, her heart leaping, but he gave her no chance to speak.

"We shall dine very shortly, but a visit to my Aunt Regina is of primary importance."

"Lady Regina?" Polly's eyes flew wide in alarm. "But I feel she's distinctly averse to me, Sir Richard, and when she learns of my truancy – "

"Nonsense, Regina's never set store by convention, so stop looking like a scared rabbit. Her health is much improved since last you were here and she awaits you with pleasure."

Polly thought this very unlikely and with a sinking feeling followed him upstairs. As far as she could see, there seemed little point in prolonging her stay in this house, and what could Lady Regina possibly want with a girl like her?

The room was much as Polly remembered, with the heat now welcome, for the November air was chill. Richard led her forward to the daybed where his aunt reclined and kissing the plump hand he murmured, "Miss Polly Fielding, I'll swear, is remembered from St Michaelmas Eve."

"Dammit, Richard, I'm not a fool, of course I remember. Let the child sit beside me and, knowing my wishes, I trust you'll leave us undisturbed."

Timidly Polly sat facing the woman as Richard retired. She was baffled at the kindly behaviour of one previously so churlish.

"Good Heavens, girl, you look decidedly pale. Am I sugh an ogre?"

Tremulously Polly shook her head. "I'm not exactly a child, you know."

"Old enough to tolerate an old woman's whims? I'm known as the witch of St Mary's, are you aware of that?"

Remembering rumours and giggles from Arabella's friends, Polly forced herself to answer firmly. "I would say such tales are unfounded, my lady."

"Oh, fie! The most atrocious ones are true, but Prinny was kind and generous, a great lover in his day. I wept forgotten tears when the guns told of his death. There'll never be the likes of him again. That William is a drivelling fool; did you set eyes on him in London?"

"Not once; I'm told he shuns the public."

The rouged mouth opposite set in disapproval and the fleeting wistfulness was gone as she keenly peered into Polly's face.

"I understand you walked all the way from London. Is Frances Lloyd not to your liking?"

"She was very good to me, but – "

"Not the best of company, I'll warrant. You were sent to her in disgrace, I believe."

Polly smiled faintly. "Well, on the night of the ball – "

"I am quite aware of those amusing events and only regret not being present to witness the shock you caused."

"I meant no harm and now feel ashamed. The Hamiltons showed me great kindness and I repaid them so disgracefully. You see no one expected to see me, a sort of superior servant, at the ball. I had climbed above my station."

"Servant be damned! Don't humble yourself, it does not become such as you. You are young, my dear, and far too gullible."

"I was eighteen years old last month."

"I know your exact age, child, and a great deal more about you than you know yourself."

"Do you?" Eagerly Polly sat forward. "Do you, Lady Regina?"

"Cease fussing for a moment and answer me one more question. Is there aught between you and my nephew?"

The girl caught her breath at the abrupt question. "Sir Richard has been most considerate."

"But not more – no more?"

Biting her lip in embarrassment Polly felt herself flushing but she returned the other's look coolly.

"I don't understand your question, Lady Regina."

"Well, no matter. There's a small casket under the window, kindly bring it to me, Mary."

At her startled glance the old lady smiled. "You must be aware your name is Mary. What girl was ever christened Polly?"

She took the beautiful casket inlaid with precious gems, and unlocking it, opened the lid to reveal a nest of jewels. Her podgy fingers delved among the contents, bringing out an oval miniature in a narrow gold frame. Thrusting it under the girl's nose her eyes narrowed thoughtfully.

"Take a close look at it, child. That girl was your mother."

Polly did not doubt the words as she gazed at the exquisite painting. It might have been her own face smiling there, her own green eyes, her own red hair, although longer, curling in ringlets about the white shoulders.

She could scarcely breathe for excitement. Her mother, this enchanting, delicate-looking creature, and her questioning eyes turned to the other woman, who nodded soberly.

"Remember the ball? It is surely not surprising the elders almost fainted with shock; your face was the reason for such a furore. A ghost stood before them, the ghost of dead Caroline Mary, famed throughout the county for her looks."

"Caroline Mary Wintringham?"

With sudden alertness Regina sat up.

"You know of her?"

"Not exactly, but I found her grave in the garden of that old burnt-out house. I feel so bewildered and ignorant of my birth; please be good enough to enlighten me."

"Caroline Mary was the Rector's only child, the most delightful creature for miles. Every buck in the county made a play for her and she led them a pretty dance."

"But she died at eighteen."

"Sadly she did, when giving birth to you. A tragic

tale, one of many, no marriage, no husband, you understand.''

Polly sat with her eyes on the picture. "And my father?"

"Who knows? Accusation and rumour aplenty ran rife but God curse all males, it's the woman who pays. Your grandfather, Joshua Wintringham, was as pious a devil as ever lived and as mean a one. It was rumoured he had wealth, but in his thirty years among us spent not a penny on the Rectory, nor on his daughter. No wonder the child went astray, she was spoilt and acclaimed by everyone in the county to atone for her father's neglect. But he had his revenge by imprisoning her in the Rectory when her condition became known. They say she died in agony at your birth and was buried at night in the garden.''

Tears sprang to Polly's eyes. "Oh, don't, please don't."

"It's useless to weep for the past, my dear. Thank God for your own life and John Hamilton's common sense. He was your grandfather's lawyer and whether from compassion or devious means of his own, he claimed responsibility for the deserted brat you were. He boarded you out with the Fieldings, farmers at Budleigh.''

Polly frowned in contemplation. "A few years at most. I was four when attending school in Bath.''

"I know nothing of that, neither had I thought to set eyes on you in my life. On St Michaelmas night, when Richard presented you, my shock matched that of others.''

The girl's eyes glowed. "I thought my presence offended you, but how absurd it all seems now. Thank you, dear Lady Regina, for being so honest with me. I fear I've greatly misjudged the Hamiltons and must make immediate amends."

"Fiddlesticks, let them stew. It would please me if you'd stay here for a while. Life is lonely with only a neglectful nephew for company."

"Does Richard know about my mother?"

"He knows more than is good for him, no doubt. Leave him be child, probe no further, you ask too many questions."

She sank into her cushions and Polly crept hesitantly from the room, her mind in a whirl. Joy at discovering her mother, at proving her affinity with Caroline Mary, engulfed her, but bewilderment and sadness mingled at such an unhappy tale. She crept about the great house in a daze, listening for the sound of Richard's horse, torn between an urge to rush to the neglected grave, trim the grass and plant sweet-scented flowers, and walking towards Stoke House, there to humbly beg pardon of the man to whom she owed her life.

Wandering into the garden, misty and chill, as the sea winds blew, she walked in confusion until Richard appeared and asked without preamble, "Is the tale told?"

"Much of it, yes. The joy of owning a name and finding a mother as lovely as Caroline Mary has overwhelmed me."

"She were never more beautiful than her daughter."

Her eyes sought his face quickly but she read nothing there to raise her hopes and stifling a sigh she continued. "Your aunt is lonely, Richard, but I cannot stay. I owe Mr Hamilton an untold debt and apologies for the trouble I've caused will never suffice. I can see now my aversion to Stoke House was quite unjustified and I'd like to return there as soon as possible."

"Very well, I'll escort you myself. I have business to discuss with John Hamilton, a marriage is in the offing."

She felt the colour drain from her face as she strove to control her voice. "How soon?"

"The day is not fixed. You must ask Arabella."

He would not meet her eyes and strode away as if every devil in hell followed him. What a complex man he was, secret, brooding, brusque and unpredictable, determined, it seemed on marriage with Arabella and yet, during the last few hours, kind and considerate to herself, a lost, unhappy girl. But did she want his kindness when once she had his love, a love that apparently had faded in him to something not worthy of mention.

Seven

As they drove to Stoke House he seemed withdrawn and distant, as if unwilling to become involved in her problems. But when they arrived he took her arm encouragingly. Firmly Polly withdrew it.

"I am no longer afraid of anyone now I answer to Miss Wintringham and although still penniless, I dare say I'll survive. Will you be good enough to allow me to meet them alone?"

On entering the house, in spite of such brave words, she felt slightly nervous and was relieved to encounter Arabella immediately.

"Polly!" The dark girl cried, overcome with shock. "Oh, thank goodness you are home."

Flushing with surprise, her timidity fading, Polly smiled hopefully.

"Does that mean I'm welcome and, I hope, forgiven? A chance to apologise for my shameful behaviour is all I ask."

"You'd better sit down and tell me all about it. Since learning of your disappearance we've been very concerned and Papa is most upset. Not very pleased with your behaviour, I fear."

"I'm almost afraid to meet him, but many things have come to light, Arabella, and I feel sure he will understand." She played nervously with the ribbons on her bonnet, and keeping her voice deliberately casual, continued, "I believe congratulations are in order. I do hope you'll find much happiness."

"Thank you. It is exciting isn't it, and I feel quite overcome. May I ask how you learned the news?"

It was clear Richard's carriage had departed unobserved, but before Polly could reply, John Hamilton himself joined them. She noticed how his face cleared on seeing her and instantly he loudly exclaimed, "So you've returned at last."

She sat silent awaiting his outburst but when he spoke it was with natural calm. "You are in good health, I presume, and aware of the trouble you've caused us all?"

"I beg your pardon for past misdemeanours and hope you will forgive me, Mr Hamilton. I deeply regret the way I've repaid Mrs Lloyd's kindness, but would it surprise you to learn I was homesick?"

"Homesick, Miss Fielding, for a place you know so little of?"

"It is enough that my roots are here, I have no doubt you, too, are aware of that. Neither do I now answer to Miss Fielding."

The colour faded from Hamilton's face and he sank into a chair. Arabella looked on with alarm. "Are you ill, Papa, perhaps a glass of wine – "

Irritably, he waved a feeble hand, while he and Polly faced each other.

"Would you kindly explain those remarks," he asked.

Briefly and precisely Polly told her tale, omitting nothing she felt the other should know. Her own simple language, abundantly clear, found Hamilton wiping his glistening face and Arabella open-mouthed with astonishment.

When the man found his voice it was heavy. "You heard that tale from Lady Regina's lips and have no reason to doubt her word?"

"None. She has a portrait of my mother, we are very much alike."

"That is perfectly true. Evan as a child the resemblance was uncanny."

"Oh, Mr Hamilton!" Polly rose and placed her hand involuntarily on his arm. "How can I ever express my thanks? Only your goodness gave me a chance to live and I'm never likely to forget that."

Arabella broke in with exasperation. "I do wish one of you would remember I'm here and explain this rigmarole."

"You shall hear it all, my dear, in time," her father rebuked before turning to Polly. "And you, my dear, are puzzled by such secrecy, I presume?"

"Well, it does seem odd that you brought me into your house yet kept me ignorant of my birth. Surely I had a right to know."

He passed a hand across his face before glancing at his daughter. "Perhaps Miss Wintringham would like you to leave us."

Polly shook her head and at his request removed her outdoor things. He sat her comfortably, facing him, smiling ruefully.

"I would rather the truth had been learnt from me but I delayed too long. There is no need to repeat the painful facts of which you are aware, but I must explain that as Joshua Wintringham's lawyer I felt responsibility towards you at his desertion. With the passing of your childhood my obligations ceased although the fact that Arabella liked you naturally pleased me, and bringing you into Stoke House as my daughter's companion was a solution I've never regretted.

"The secret of your birth was kept with the best intentions, and when the time was ripe I intended revealing the necessary information. I would point out that if licentious behaviour is permissible in larger cities, a small community like ours still has scruples, and illegitimacy, on the whole, is condemned. Your grandfather suffered so unmercifully, he never survived the disgrace inflicted on him by your mother. Her shameful conduct destroyed him."

"Poor girl," Polly cried passionately, "so disowned she lies forgotten in a garden wilderness. Well, I welcome her to my life, Mr Hamilton, and am proud to be her daughter! But as I so resemble her did not the risk of recognition trouble you?"

"Not necessarily. I doubt if young folk in this town have ever heard of Caroline Mary, neither would their mothers refer to such a distasteful case, now best forgotten. Only a few veterans remember the incident, as you've already learnt to your sorrow."

"But – "

"No 'buts', my dear, it is over now and I welcome you back to my house."

Gratitude and warmth flowed through Polly for this man with so generous a heart. Arabella came forward, a ghost of a smile on her face.

"I see there is much I have to learn, and await the telling with impatience. But I, too, am glad you are back, Polly dear, there's so much to do for my wedding and you have such excellent notions."

Hamilton sighed with contentment and something like relief. "A feather in my daughter's cap for winning the catch of the county, don't you agree? As mistress of St Mary's Manor her friendship towards you will put a stop to wagging tongues and very likely bring elegible suitors." He paused with a wistful glance at Polly. "There was a time when I felt you favoured Hugo. Was I too ambitious?"

"Ambitious?" She laughed, "Why Hugo could pick from a dozen girls. As for myself, I have no wish to marry."

"Not at present perhaps, but the day will come."

"Oh, Papa," Arabella cried, her dark eyes sparkling. "what a romantic you are. But please excuse us now, there is a great deal to discuss."

Once more installed in Stoke House, Polly's life changed quite drastically. She became Arabella's closest confidante and endless chatter of a trousseau and future plans ensued. The Caldwell girls were much in evidence, agog with curiosity about Polly's strange story and slightly perplexed at the pride with which her new name was acclaimed. The sad, indelicate details of the tale were savoured with delight, the once inferior Polly now regarded with some awe.

But for all their new amiability Polly longed for Lucy's return, perhaps to gain courage from her friend's never-failing ebullience. Now that a date in

February was fixed for the wedding she accepted the inevitable as calmly as possible, but much of the sparkle had gone from her life and in Richard's company, which was avoided whenever possible, she shrank into a silent shell. It was not difficult to evade him, for he seemed purposely to shun her and on social occasions they scarcely exchanged a word.

In spite of icy winds now sweeping the clifftop, Polly made a point of visiting the Rectory to tend her mother's grave. Surprisingly enough, Hugo offered his help, and armed with tools borrowed from the gardener's shed, they cleared a neat patch, setting bulbs to flower in spring. Polly collected pebbles to decorate the border, deriving satisfaction from her finished work.

An urge to enter the ruined house was discouraged by Hugo, who declared the rotten timbers dangerous and the smell of decay unwholesome.

During the month of December, when Stoke House bustled with activity, and the wedding occupied many thoughts, Polly was glad to escape, riding the ponderous cob over the rain-washed heather. She found Hugo's company pleasant and balm to her embittered heart, for he obviously admired her, and old feuds forgotten, they shared a new-found trust. But she knew the day would come when a proposal could not be avoided. She also knew without doubt that were the idea of marriage not repugnant to her, such a union was out of the question. Although an amusing companion, Hugo's breezy nature was fickle, and Polly, unfashionably droll, expected a faithful husband.

Apart from such deliberations there was Lucy to consider and sometimes Polly persuaded her to join them in a gallop. But the tall girl, normally so calm and self-assured, became gauche and silent in Hugo's company and he failed to see how brilliantly she could shine or the laughter her witticisms caused. Determined, however, to further her friend's cause, Polly persevered only to be dismayed by Hugo's proposal when caught unawares.

Firmly and with finality, it was refused and the young man's look of hurt and displeasure amused her. She felt he would never grieve long over any woman and teasingly she chided, "Come, Hugo, where is your good humour and the nonchalance expected of a repulsed suitor?"

"I don't feel the least amused by your refusal, Polly. I'm deuced miserable and fear you favour another. Is that so?"

"Certainly not, I have not the slightest inclination to marry. But your father would welcome your own marriage and there are many willing takers, I'm sure."

"If you refer to those obnoxious Caldwell girls," he answered sourly, "I'd as soon remain a bachelor for ever."

She laughed and suggested with sly unconcern. "Well, what about Lucy Carmichael? She may not have looks but her style is faultless, she's fun and the cleverest girl for miles."

"You don't have to sing Lucy's praises, neither am I fooled by your devious hints. I have known the girl too long and I'm perfectly aware she's in love with me, so a fig to your matchmaking."

"You really are quite insufferable and Lucy is far too good for you. But it seems you are lacking in sense when discarding such a prize so casually. You may very well dally too long, there are others eager to marry Lucy, if only for her money."

She felt no guilt at her fabrication when she saw the gleam in his eye and his head rise alertly. "Others – what others?"

"Not necessarily of these parts, but you are surely aware how often the Carmichaels travel and good-looking males abound throughout England. Lucy will surprise us all one day, I've no doubt."

It gave her immense satisfaction to see discomfort appear on the arrogant face, coupled with a preoccupied frown. She hoped the seeds of doubt and perplexity sown in his head might bring fruition in the shape of an offer for Lucy's hand. Whether her friend accepted such a hazardous adventure as marriage with the capricious Hugo was her affair, but at least the chance of refusing him would give her satisfaction.

Christmas came, mild and wet, for snow fell rarely in Devon. Geese were fattened and garlands made to mingle with holly and ivy decorating Stoke House.

Oliver came home from school, taller and full of confidence. He was never at a loss for words, though rarely in the house, finding a new friend in the rowdy stable-boy. He treated Polly to the scant attention bestowed on the whole family and ruefully she thought of the letters she had penned, realising how unnecessary they would be in the future.

On the whole, time passed pleasantly enough but there was bitterness in one man's eyes as he watched Polly cavorting with Hugo, a bitterness stifled by fear and a black fury that settled in his heart. Purposely he kept his distance, but one day they met quite by chance. She was alone, but had obviously put the cob to a gallop, for her colour was high and hair in damp ringlets about her face. They drew rein simultaneously and she half smiled at his dour face.

"It amazes me," he remarked coolly, "to see you happily alone. You seem to find young Hamilton's company quite stimulating."

"I certainly do, my dear Richard, my riding has improved tremendously thanks to Hugo's help. I sometimes wonder what happened to that little steed you once suggested I try. Minnie is getting a trifle old and too fat."

Ignoring his wooden silence she went on. "Sometimes we ride along the shore but the sea is cold now and Minnie objects." She looked past him to the sullen grey waves and her voice dropped to a near-whisper. "But I never go down at night now, Richard, never when the moon is full."

Neither heeded the lightly falling rain as they sat refusing to meet each other's eyes, then suddenly he growled disagreeably.

"Hugo is over-familiar, I think, and not to my liking."

"Your liking? Is the way I conduct myself any concern of yours, Sir Richard? It was not my intention to recall the past, forgive me for that, but the day you deserted me for Arabella you forfeited any place in my life. I object to the criticism of my friends and I'll thank you to keep out of my affairs."

The wintry light revealed his glittering eyes but she failed to notice how white were the knuckles gripping his reins or how her nearness choked him.

Swinging aside, he thundered away across the sodden turf and in angry bewilderment Polly trotted home recalling his boorish remarks. Could this be the man she had once gambolled so freely with on the shore, the man whose husky voice had called her his dear little mermaid and kissed away her hurt? Could this be he who had cosseted her when weary and forlorn, the Richard who had wrenched the heart out of her?

The thought of staying to see him wed another was painful, but without causing gossip she had little choice. Somehow her wits must be put to further use, for although nothing remained to keep her in this town, she had no wish to leave the county, and later she hoped a living could be sought outside the proximity of St Mary's Manor. The small, select towns along the coast surely held many possibilities.

There was a strange infrequency about Richard's visits to Stoke House which did not pass unnoticed, but Arabella apparently felt no qualms that her betrothed was a laggard lover. She firmly believed her own person the cause, and prattled confidentially to her friends.

"Richard finds anticipation a stimulus and is impatient to wed. He is busily preparing the Manor suitably for a bride. I have told him of my wishes regarding our quarters and workmen are engaged in carrying out this work."

"How long is it since you were there, Arabella?"

"Not since the ball, as a matter of fact. I don't care for Lady Regina and until I set foot inside as Richard's wife, I prefer to keep my distance. The new decorations in my favourite colours will be entirely satisfactory, I'm sure, and I've no hesitation in leaving the details to Richard. The older part of the house doesn't interest me, it's far too gloomy for my liking, with those miserable tattered old hangings, but I shall have to learn to live with them, I suppose. Later, when children are born, I'll insist on greater alterations, for Richard would not wish his heirs infected with such cheerlessness."

Polly's thoughts turned to Lady Regina. Much as

she had wished to revisit that lady, the probability of now doing so seemed impossible.

"You've not met the tiresome old thing since your betrothal?" asked Clarissa.

"Not once, I'm pleased to say, and I've no idea how she feels about our marriage. I doubt a new mistress in her home will be taken kindly."

"She's fond of Richard, I believe, and would like to see him happy, I'm sure."

"Perhaps you're right. Polly saw her quite recently and can answer your questions better than I."

Several pairs of eyes turned to Polly and she smiled. "I feel you misjudge the old lady, she showed me nothing but kindness. I think she was probably lovely before becoming so gross. The dropsy has made her very ill."

"Then perhaps her days are numbered, I hope so for everyone's sake."

"Oh, Arabella, how can you say such a dreadful thing?"

"There's no point in being hypocritical, Richard has been a trifle moody of late and I'm sure his aunt is the cause. No matter, in less than two weeks we'll be wed and I'm so glad you returned in good time, Polly dear. Papa will be lonely when I am gone, and he and Hugo are not exactly compatible."

"So must I be the go-between? I have no intention of living any longer than necessary on your father's charity. Plenty of wealthy families reside in this county and one of them might possibly require a governess. I have experience enough at teaching, heaven knows."

"You mean to earn your own keep?" asked a scandalised voice.

"Well, I think it's a splendid idea," Lucy retorted

quickly. "Many a harassed parent would jump at such a treasure, and I'm only too pleased you've decided to stay in the county."

Arabella was thoughtful after the other girls left. Her usual calm seemed ruffled, and her face set when Polly enquired the cause.

"There's nothing wrong exactly, but I think it unwise to consider a situation at the moment, Polly. Papa, I am sure, will strongly object and very shortly I believe great changes might occur."

Polly looked at her with puzzled eyes. "You talk in riddles sometimes, Arabella."

"Perhaps I should not disclose Papa's secrets but I'd not feel happy at leaving Stoke House without warning you about certain events which can only prove advantageous."

"I do wish you'd get to the point. How can your father's affairs affect me?"

"Quite a lot, as it happens. You know Rector Wintringham was your grandfather but are you aware how rich a man he was? All he possessed was left in trust until you reach a certain age. Exactly what age I'm unable to say, but it must be fairly soon."

Polly was filled with disbelief. "Are you telling me the truth, Arabella?"

"Indeed I am. The news surprises and delights me too, although I learned it purely by accident. Papa is your guardian, you see, and when he was preparing my dowry I stumbled upon this extraordinary document. He has no idea I discovered it, of course, and I feel that did he know his anger would be great. But don't you see, Polly, how it alters your position? There's no need to rush away to care for tiresome children. Simply be patient for a while."

The news, if true, filled Polly with a quiet wonder

and she sat almost subconsciously reflecting on her earlier life. All those years in Bath, the hardships and privations, the humility and gratitude, had been nothing but a farce and she owed so very little to the Hamiltons.

She looked into Arabella's face, which was smooth now but showed concern, as she continued. "You must not blame my father for keeping you in ignorance. I dare say he had his reasons and when the time comes, all will be explained. But I trust you won't betray me, dear."

Unable to speak, Polly shook her head and going towards the other girl, kissed her gently.

"I'll never do that," she said at last, "but thank you for telling me. Somehow it all seems like a dream, are you sure there is no mistake!"

"Quite sure."

"Do you think, knowing my grandfather's secretive ways, others might speculate?"

"Most unlikely, he was a man to be shunned although the whole town knows by now you are Caroline Mary's daughter."

"Is it possible Hugo suspects?"

"Good heavens, no! Hugo sees little of what goes on under his nose."

"In that case, I'll be happy to stay until your father sees fit to confide in me." Polly caressed the lace wedding gown stretched on the bed and thought of her mother, young and lovely, alone in her extremity with no vows to atone for her child. "Would it be possible to discover my father's identity?" she asked.

"I doubt it. Papa believes such probings to be indelicate but privately I feel he is as foxed as everyone else. The girl was faithful to her lover, even in death."

Such a tragedy was never far from Polly's mind but

forthcoming independence filled her with elation and no longer did the future appear a time to dread.

She regarded the Hamiltons with greater affection, Arabella's former truculence forgotten, for now she was akin to them. Every penny spent, every mouthful of food she ate, should one day be repaid a thousandfold.

Her impatient longing for the coming expectations made life difficult and only her vow to Arabella prevented a confidential outburst to Lucy.

Hours were spent at the Carmichaels' farm and, forsaking Hugo, she hopefully awaited his move towards her friend. That it came a few days before the wedding when she saw them meet on a misty horizon gave Polly immense satisfaction and she turned back to Stoke House alone.

Entering the house a strange quiet, at variance with the present activity, struck her as unusual and opening the sitting-room door she found Arabella and her father in sombre mood. The tears on her friend's lashes were instantly apparent and Polly ran forward impulsively. At her enquiring eyes Hamilton spoke soberly. "Sad news I'm afraid from the Manor."

"St Mary's?" Polly whispered, her heart thudding.

"Lady Regina died this morning, not unexpected, I suppose, but Richard is quite distraught. It means the wedding must be postponed for the present."

As she comforted the weeping Arabella, Polly's treacherous heart soared, for in spite of a feeling of sadness for poor lonely Regina, her death seemed like a reprieve. With a feeling of genuine regret, however, she turned to Arabella.

"We must go to Budleigh and offer our help. Richard will need us."

"It is not his wish," the other replied. "He

particularly asked to be left alone, which I find most hurtful. Surely my place is by his side and although I had no affection for Lady Regina I understand the pull of family ties." She began to sob loudly. "I find such disruption of my plans too hard to bear and now everyone will expect me to be gloomy and miserable when secretly I feel quite unmoved. I simply cannot bear it."

Sensing hysteria, Polly sympathetically led the unhappy girl to her bed, where, with hot milk laced with brandy, she soon fell asleep.

Still wearing her riding-clothes, Polly left the house and walked purposefully towards the shore, unaware of the icy wind whipping about her habit as she walked slowly on the newly washed sand. Her heart ached for Richard, alone with his grief in that great sombre house. Only she knew of his love for his aunt, his tenderness towards the gross, pathetic old lady and the emnity between them now seemed mean and futile. She turned and looked towards Budleigh, willing her compassion to reach the silent Manor, when suddenly she saw him sitting immobile, outlined against the winter sky. Wrapped in his cloak, the handsome dark head bent in sadness, choked her.

"Richard," she faltered tremulously, "Richard."

Slowly he rose and turned towards her. "Polly, I might have known."

She held out her hands and he took them, keeping her at arms length, stiff and unbending and the impulse to throw herself against his chest subsided.

"I had to come, my dear, I am so sorry."

"It was considerate of you."

"Considerate? Oh, Richard, I know what she meant to you. Mother and father, you told me once, the kindest woman on earth to a small bewildered boy.

I'm never likely to forget those words, and if it will ease your pain, simply talk to me about her. I have no other comfort to offer."

They stood together gazing without hope into each other's eyes, then he nodded. "Walk with me for a while, that's all I ask."

He strode along facing the wind and without comment her rapid feet kept pace with his. Slowly she felt the tenseness subside and relaxation flow in every limb while his nearness brought her exquisite pain. She knew for the rest of her life how these precious, fleeting moments would be treasured.

At last, with agitation gone, he stopped by the path to Stoke House and looked down on her damp, bare head. Her breath in little foggy clouds seemed to make him, for the first time, aware of her.

"Dearest Polly, I cannot thank you enough, simply for your presence. Life has been difficult for both of us lately and was never more so than now. Forgive my disgraceful behaviour towards you, but soon all will be explained. Aunt Regina left a token for you and I prefer to hand it to you myself. Come to the Manor alone as soon after the funeral as possible."

"Do you think that's wise?"

"I do. Now please excuse me."

She nodded and watched him out of sight, while the afternoon light faded over the sea. Forlornly she saw it vanish like her impossible dream, leaving her lost and frightened and terribly in love with the man promised in honour to her own best friend.

Eight

Polly sat with a miniature in either hand. One she knew as her mother, but the other, similarly framed in gold, was of an unknown gentleman. His mischievous eyes and arrogant mouth smiled mockingly and she looked at Richard in bewilderment as he offered her a sealed scroll.

"Although addressed to you," he said, "I am aware of the contents. You may read it here if you wish, but I shall understand should you care to do so in privacy."

She glanced around at the opulent luxury that had once been Lady Regina's room. No longer was it filled with suffocating heat, for a sharp, salty breeze blew through the open windows. Two days ago the old matriarch had been laid to rest in the family vault, the last of a dying age, thought Polly, whose intuition told her what changes would follow. It was possible that Richard would discard much of the unnecessary clutter, retaining only the best of his inheritance. A new date for the wedding was not yet fixed, but Arabella, now reverting to her old calm self, realised she could afford to bide her time. No tiresome old resident at the Manor could now disrupt her life and she had every intention of livening the dreary place up, with taste and discretion naturally, after the weeks of mourning.

Placing the two pictures together on a small table, Polly took up the letter. "I'd prefer to read it now if you please," she said quietly.

"Of course." He moved towards the door. "I shall wait in the study across the hall."

"Must you go? Your presence does not disturb me."

"I think it better so."

Alone, with some trepidation, she opened the parchment scroll. "My dear Caroline Mary," it began and confused for a moment she faltered, before smiling at her own absurdity. The letter was addressing her Caroline Mary Wintringham.

"The miniature of your mother," she read on, "must find its rightful place in your possession. Treasure it with pride and never condemn her, for she was ill used.

"The uniform picture will undoubtedly fox you, but study the handsome face carefully, my dear, for the eyes and the turn of the saucy head will be familiar. This is my brother Ambrose, and Richard's father. A rake without conscience but lovable, none the less, as many a weak woman found to her sorrow. It will shock you to learn he was the Wintringham girl's lover and with something akin to sorrow I present to you, your father!

"I am indeed a degenerate old woman but Richard is dear to me and the pain he suffered when the truth of your birth was revealed well nigh destroyed him. For months I kept him under oath regarding the matter, feeling your true identity should be told at my discretion. Perhaps concealment was a cruel whim of mine but I refused to give gossips the satisfaction of denouncing Ambrose. After my death it will matter no more.

"I do trust, however, for Richard's sake, the chapter

is now closed. Keep the mutual affection between you, but remember, above all things, he is your brother. You both have pride, and during our fleeting acquaintance I sensed the strength of your character. You have enough to face a pitiless situation without faltering.

"Ever your affectionate

Regina Anne Meredith."

Sorrow, some anger, but above all, a searing clarity swept through Polly as she put aside the letter and gazed at the bright, bold picture. Illegitimacy had never troubled her, but a curiosity about her father had naturally persisted. Now the pleasure of knowing his identity was tinged with a frightening bitterness. The fact that Richard, whom she admittedly loved, was her brother threw a blinding light on many an unknown problem. She readily understood his revulsion of their forbidden mutual attraction, realising only his marriage to Arabella would save them. Dear, beloved Richard, the agony of losing him could now be borne with fortitude.

At the sound of his footsteps she turned and smiling through faint tears, faced him shyly.

"Oh, Richard. I've never had a brother before, help me to appreciate you."

"Don't you think I need support too? You know of my love and nothing can disclaim it. One cannot blame an old woman for her deception, the fault lies with me for being so insensible."

"What sin was there except ignorance? We are both creatures of circumstance and the only possible way out has already been taken. How sensibly you acted in proposing to Arabella, she'll make you a good wife and the Manor a fine mistress, far better than I, who have little finesse."

"You've every right to change things if you wish and take your rightful place here as did Regina."

"What nonsense you talk! Her wish to keep my father's name secret fails to trouble me and I'm quite prepared to abide by her decision." She laughed suddenly. "If all were told, what a ludicrous situation could arise from this. But think how embarrassed we both should be and how scandalised Arabella!"

Soberly she looked seriously into his face. "To the folk in this town and the Hamiltons I am still the bastard child of Caroline Mary, and happy to keep it that way. Further speculation can only do harm and as long as only we two know the truth it concerns no other."

"Nevertheless, you shall be financially secure and no longer dependent on others."

Polly bit her lip, but the promise made to Arabella must be honoured and she could not disclose her future expectations.

"Lucy Carmichael has plans for me," she answered quickly. "She is a dear friend and I am happy in her company. I intend leaving Stoke House shortly after your marriage, if that eases your mind."

He calmly surveyed her but spoke with a touch of irony. "You are very considerate but I'm not anxious to shirk my responsibilities."

"Oh come, you're being too solemn and extremely pompous with me."

Laughing a lighthearted laugh too long absent, her green eyes glowed with warmth. She longed to put her arms about him and see the troubled face relax, but both were aware of dangerous gestures, realising time was needed for a harmless family relationship to develop between them.

It was the fashion to treat emotions casually and

marriage as a convenient arrangement. Such an attitude suited Richard admirably, for he had never declared ardent love for Arabella, neither, he believed, was it expected, for the girl seemed perfectly satisfied with their cordial understanding.

His life had been remarkably free from entanglements with never a serious love until Polly, with her elf-like movements, had enraptured him. His forced casual treatment of her cost him dear, the hurt puzzlement in her eyes over a reproach and destroying the imploring letters from London left the acrid smell of burning in his nostrils for days. At times he found difficulty in treating with kindness the aunt, who had, with her revelations, destroyed his dream. But cursing an ironic fate did nothing to ease the ache in his heart for what could never be, and relief at sharing the secret with Polly was simply a finality.

Now, life must go on, and the wedding plans be resumed. He was not unaware of Arabella's charms, popular throughout the county and capable of residing graciously as lady of the Manor, in addition to providing, he hoped, heirs to continue the Meredith line.

To Polly, it was a time of transition while she viewed an unknown future with impatience and some regret. She visualised a new, exciting life with the aid of her expected inheritance and travel now figured largely among her plans. The world held many treasures for her eyes to see and these could surely lift the weight from her heart.

She found it increasingly difficult to regard Richard as a brother and, as long as there was contact between them, strong illicit emotions remained. In all fairness to them both and Arabella, she knew the greatest distance between them was the only solution.

So much for remaining in Devon. She had no choice now but to go far away and fast-growing America, with its new bustling towns, was even considered.

A decent interval had passed since Lady Regina's death and it was evident the marriage should no longer be postponed.

Polly, in an agony of indecision, awaited John Hamilton's disclosures regarding her inheritance. Naturally, the wedding was very much on his mind but she chafed at the delay, refusing to discuss a money settlement with Richard until he returned from his honeymoon in London, a reasonable enough excuse.

As fresh April winds blew in from the sea, it seemed impossible that nearly a year had passed since she first set foot in Stoke House. Now, familiar with the county, many hours were spent riding alone, for Hugo had deserted her and often was espied in Lucy's company. While rejoicing at the success of her manoeuvres Polly missed her absent friends acutely, feeling without resentment the irony of life.

Riding alone one evening the sight of nesting birds busily darting to and fro in the density of the old Rectory garden compelled her to dismount. Her mother's grave, now tended regularly, glowed with gillyflowers and late daffodils, but in spite of her many visits, the house itself had only once been entered. She had crept carefully about the ground-floor rooms, touching the delapidated furniture covered with a film of dust.

Now, in spite of the fading light, she entered the house again, expertly dodging giant cobwebs which hung in profusion and tangled with the mildewed curtains. She crossed to the staircase never before attempted, and slowly began to ascend, while glancing curiously at the faded portraits seen in a ghostly light. She felt no fear, only exaltation when reaching the top, doors were pushed open and every room scanned. All was still and forlorn, the beds standing vacant as though no living creature had ever rested there.

Bolder now, she opened closet doors to see garments faded and riddled with moth. No suggestion of femininity lingered, no faint whiff of perfume, fans or slippers, no forgotten gowns. There was not a single trace of Caroline Mary, she might never have lived in this unhappy house.

Turning away to descend the stairs, a small door on the landing caught Polly's attention. It took little effort to force the rusty bolt and behind the door rose a narrow, twisting staircase. Ever curious, she climbed them and came to a large attic under the eaves where remnants of bygone days intrigued her. Strange little toys and stiff powdered wigs proclaimed a link with the past and her hands touched the pathetic abandoned things with affection. She found fascination in a painted sedan chair, the interior padded with Parisian elegance in faded pink silk. She opened the door to receive the smell of musk and could not resist climbing cautiously inside.

Although so slight, her added weight was enough to send the chair with startling suddenness through the decaying floorboards. Dazed and frightened, she was brought to quick recovery by pain and a trickle of blood, and with it came the realisation she was trapped inside the cab, her legs held fast in the door. The chair sloped at an alarming angle with rear poles firmly wedged in the splintered floor and any effort to release herself might well bring about disaster. Being flung to the depths below was a terrifying thought but little damage to herself was suffered, merely a bruised leg, possibly cut, although certainly not broken.

Frustration at her helpless position gradually subsided and sensibly she suppressed the urge to shout. No one could possibly hear her cries except patient Minnie tied in the overgrown lane and the chance of a passing traveller was remote. It might be hours before she was found, and with as little disturbance as possible, she tried to settle herself in a comfortable spot, prepared to wait for deliverance.

Smoothing the silk lining of her prison some time was passed in visualising the occupants of such an elegant chair. Very likely her ancestors and possibly her own mother had ridden in style in this very vehicle, but, on reflection, the latter seemed highly improbable. Even twenty years ago the chair would be out of date, although the thought of her mother creeping up to this lonely attic to dream her prohibited dreams was possible.

The thought brought a smile while her hand subconsciously stroked the padding, when a faint rustle beneath the silk made her pause and she noticed an almost invisible slit. With no trouble at all she ripped the panel down and her eager fingers closed quickly over a package before it slithered out of reach.

The gloomy light could not conceal the bundle of letters she held, tied tightly with a length of fraying ribbon, and peering closely, Polly fancied the handwriting appeared somewhat childish. But it was now too dark to decipher the contents and she sat with the bundle clasped in her hand as she waited through the long night to be rescued. A faint indescribable scent rose from the letters, to fill her with a strange excitement too intense for dismissal.

Sleep was difficult, for a shutter flapped eerily in the

wind, and she welcomed the morning light filtering through the broken skylight. A fresh morning breeze brought a couple of cheerful robins for company as she rubbed her cramped arms, then the letters resting on her knee banished all tedium, and carefully, with anticipation, she pulled away the ribbon and started to read.

Expecting to find simple love letters she was unprepared for the passionate desire flowing across each page as the writer poured out her heart to her lover. Polly flinched now and then at prying into such intimacies but somehow she felt no surprise to see the signature of Caroline Mary, and it soon became clear they were penned to a man called Theodore Spring. Each one was dated through the summer of 1812 and addressed to 'My darling Theo'.

Methodically she read the letters until one, distinctly different and obviously written by a male hand, surprised her. The morning sun had risen higher making the words quite clear, and dismissing his tender preliminaries, Polly read on.

" ... I can no longer continue to deceive your father. He is a holy man, Caroline, and my conscience allows me no peace with God. I have every intention of leaving the diocese and with it temptations of the flesh. Perhaps in distant lands I shall find my salvation. You know I love you with all my heart but by overstepping convention we have sinned greatly and I bitterly regret deflowering your beauty.

"I can see no future for us together, as your father will undoubtedly oppose a marriage with his curate. He has great aspirations for you, this I know and I hereby return all your letters but not without regret. Take care, my love, and may you find happiness with one more worthy."

The letter was signed simply 'Theo' and the answering one from Caroline Mary caused Polly to quiver with excitement. The words written with apparent distress held a frantic plea that seemed to throb down the years.

" ... you cannot leave me now, Theo, when I find I am carrying your child. In spite of sick anxiety, I feel perhaps wrongfully a great exultation that our love must soon bear fruit. The secret is safe at present, not a soul in the world suspects our affair, indeed many believe I favour another, but that is not so. No other man has known me, only you, my darling Theo, can bear witness to that. Meet me tonight at our usual rendezvous, for I am near distraught and need your comfort. Do not forsake me now – "

The letter lay in Polly's hand. Had it ever been delivered or had the fright of near-discovery overcome the amorous curate? Whatever the cause a contemptible man abandoned the sorry girl heartlessly to her fate.

Soberly she gathered the letters together, her mind in confusion. This was her father, this man of God, so weak and ineffectual, she had no more pride in him than the other high-born scoundrel mistakenly offered by Lady Regina.

In her stunned bewilderment she failed to hear a shouting voice or steps on the stairs until he stood before her and then her resistance broke. The streaming face she turned to her love was filled with wonder.

"Don't fret, my dear," Richard whispered gently, "we'll soon have you out of this. Careful now, put your hands on my shoulders tightly and trust me."

He wrenched away the side of the sedan and pulled her quickly into his arms as with a sickening crash the chair disappeared below. Her moist face buried in his shoulder she listened to his calm voice praising Minnie, whose indignant snorts had attracted his attention.

Calmer now as they emerged from the house, she begged him to release her and sitting on the warm, sweet grass she allowed him to examine her leg. It seemed to be severely bruised, but impatiently she placed the faded letters in his hand.

Quick to understand her urgency, he scanned the necessary pages and when it was done looked straight into the wistful green eyes.

"You realise what this means, Polly?" he asked with husky entreaty.

Shyly she nodded. "Certainly I do. Lady Regina made a very grave error in believing we were brother and sister. It seems the penniless curate sired me and Caroline Mary loved him to distraction. Her devotion surely deserved a greater man than he."

"It's a pitiful tale, I'll allow, but will lead to a happier ending. What reason now for me to hide my love, for I do love you, Polly, with every breath I take. I thank God the truth has come to light before it's too late."

His arms were around her, his body lean and muscular, and her breathing became rapid. She clung to him enraptured as he brushed away the dust from her face with his lips and sighing, she felt contentment that was not to last long. The enormity of their behaviour made her push him abruptly away.

"Oh, Richard, what are we doing? In less than a week you will wed Arabella."

He laughed quietly at her soberness. "There will be no wedding, don't you see the fate that lured you into that house was meant to be, my darling? Arabella will have no choice but to release me."

"But she loves you, Richard. We simply cannot break her heart." Appalled she turned away. "How can we do such a dreadful thing, it's far too late."

His hands were like steel and quickly his smile faded. "Look at me, Polly," he said soberly. "Can you honestly say while believing Regina's tale you never had carnal thoughts of me? Say what is in your heart, my dear, for, wrongly or rightly, I never stopped desiring you."

She put her hands to his face in a caress. "Oh, it's true, of course it's true."

"Then no more sacrificial nonsense, if you please. I realise that Arabella will feel hurt and betrayed but I've guessed for some time that she prizes St Mary's Manor above myself. I don't doubt she cares for me as much as her heart allows, but power and position are of more importance to Arabella."

Distressed, she replied, "I think you are wrong. Everyone's known for years you would eventually marry and her father is sure to be quite distraught."

"Very likely he'll sue me for a fortune, but no matter." He kissed her and tenderly touched the bruised leg. "A poultice is needed to ease the inflamation, I'll take you to the Manor to rest while I face the hostile Hamiltons."

"You certainly will not," she cried indignantly. "You can't believe I'd shirk my part in this affair, which will surely leave us both without a shred of reputation? I have no intention of leaving you to the mercy of Arabella. We shall face it together, you and I."

"What an obstinate young woman you are, but it delights me to think our future will not be without sparks."

Nine

As they rode together towards Stoke House, Richard's grey eyes were steady, the tense lines of his face now relaxed, but Polly was flushed and with difficulty controlled thoughts that set the nerves of her stomach fluttering. For all her brave words, the thought of facing Arabella was daunting and guilt figured largely in her emotions.

It surprised her to find the Hamiltons unconcerned at her absence but as Arabella blithely explained, "We believed you were staying overnight at Lucy's home, and what a blessing Richard happened along — we must get your injured leg treated at once."

"It is nothing," Polly answered quickly, dismayed to find her voice shaking. But the warm grasp of Richard's hand on her arm gave her confidence as firmly and as gently as possible he broke the unexpected news.

A bright sun shone through the study windows and birdsong filled the air, but the four people were unaware of it, their own silence fraught with unease.

Confounded, John Hamilton sank lower into a chair, and Arabella sat like a stone, her dark eyes fixed on Polly with a frightening intensity. There might have been no one else present when she spoke at last directly to her.

"So at last you are unmasked, but not surprisingly. Your motives have always been suspect to me, I've not been blind to the mooning eyes thrown at my future husband and I should have guessed he'd be attracted by your childish ways."

The glittering eyes snapped dangerously and Richard stepped forward grimly. "Your vicious attack on Polly is quite unseemly, Arabella. Naturally you are upset, but my behaviour is the cause of that and I hold myself entirely responsible. I only regret the affair between you and I was allowed to reach such a climax, and had I told you months ago of my true feelings, such a scene could have been avoided. As it is, I can only apologise profusely, and while understanding your unhappiness must ask you to refrain from further chastising Polly. Her own regret is punishment enough."

Possessively the girl clutched his arm. "I can't believe you are so besotted, Richard. It must be a dreadful mistake. Have you forgotten our wedding takes place in three days' time?"

"It is not forgotten!" Her father rose, terrible in his anger. "Now, sir, you must answer to me for trifling with my daughter's affections. It is my intention to sue you mightily for such conduct."

"No, Papa!" I'll not be paid off like an unwanted servant. I only want the life I was led to expect, my own house and my love."

Weeping copiously now, Arabella's dejection found Polly moving towards her but savagely her arm was flung away.

"Get out of my sight, you Jezebel. I never want to see you again in my life."

Hamilton looked Polly balefully in the eye and hesitantly she glanced at Richard.

"Take no heed," he whispered leading her to the door. "Go to your room and prepare to leave the house, I'll come for you as soon as this miserable business is over."

She looked at him helplessly. "But I can't – oh, what have we done to Arabella?"

"Nothing she will not survive. I should have been firm and spared you this, now do as I ask and soon it will be over."

Finding a valise, Polly hurriedly set about collecting her things. She kept them strictly to a minimum, not wishing to be further dependent on the Hamiltons' charity. At the moment an urgency to leave Stoke House took precedence over everything, but no false move on her part should stir up unseemly gossip. Although unsure of Richard's plans, she had no intention of setting foot inside the Manor unless she did so as his wife.

The sound of quick footsteps broke into her thoughts and the door was flung open to reveal Arabella. She looked like a stranger, so aflame was her usually calm face.

"You are packing, I see. Please allow me to help, for the sooner you leave this house the better."

"Oh, Arabella, there is so much to explain – "

"The havoc you've caused to gain your own ends is explanation enough and it must give you satisfaction. I hope you realise such behaviour might spoil Richard's life, and if he weds you, Polly Fielding – which I doubt – the county will simply despise you both. While professing to be my friend you deceived me, sly as a fox, and for that you'll never be forgiven. Life at the Manor can be a lonely affair, as you'll find to your cost."

Her tempestuous words killed Polly's sympathy and

coolly she replied, "Please remember Polly Fielding
no longer exists, the poor humble foundling is now a
memory. But Caroline Mary Wintringham's reborn,
and kindly address me as such. Although at this
moment you disbelieve my regret and feel hatred for
me, Arabella, it grieves me that we part with
bitterness."

The other's eyes encountered hers levelly. "Do not
imagine the tale ends here. When Richard recovers his
senses and has tired of his new plaything, he'll cast
you aside, as any man would. Your return to a life of
poverty will be most unpleasant."

"I doubt such misfortune will happen. I have not
forgotten the inheritance you told me about yourself."

"Inheritance?" Arabella gave a mocking laugh.
"Did you really believe such a taradiddle? How
gullible you are. I'd advise you to forget it was even
mentioned."

Polly collapsed suddenly on to the bed, overcome by
the momentous events of the past hours and the
other's cutting remarks.

"Are you trying to tell me you invented the legacy?"

"Exactly. You really beg to be made a fool of, you
know."

Taking a deep breath Polly answered, "I can only
hope that one day you'll regret your cruel words,
Arabella."

"I think that very unlikely. I feel you should share
my suffering and account for your shameful
behaviour. You might have the doubtful pleasure of
owning a proper name now, but you've little else for
recommendation and I have every confidence in
reclaiming Richard's love – "

Her words were lost as she left the room and Polly
felt her head spinning with confusion and fatigue.

Arabella must surely be overcome with grief to react so violently, but when a few minutes later Richard appeared, he seemed to find nothing peculiar in her attitude.

"She's behaving with remarkable calm, my dear, but I see you are overwrought. You look so tired, my little one, and need a refreshing sleep. The Manor is noted for its comfortable beds."

"Forgive me, Richard, but I've no intention of going to St Mary's at present. Tongues will wag long enough as it is."

He smiled with rueful humour. "As you wish, it is I who must be forgiven for my thoughtlessness. No matter, we shall wed in the shortest possible time, but you cannot stay in this house, have you other plans?"

She nodded. "Take me to Lucy's home, if you please. The Carmichaels are so kind and will be sympathetic, I've not the slightest doubt." She hesitated before continuing. "Is Mr Hamilton beside himself with anger?"

"In a bit of a stew, naturally, and his blood pressure seems about to burst. Hugo appears to be off on some business of his own, but we cannot await his return."

As he sat her before him on the black horse she longed to hear more and also relate her own unpleasant interview with Arabella. But his comforting arms about her and the warm spring sunshine enfolding her in a bath of light brought the joy of a welcome sleep.

Richard rode into the Carmichaels' drive and, lifting her from the saddle with care, strode towards the porch. It was usual to find the door flung wide, for farmers are hospitable people, and the lowest vagabond was never likely to be turned away.

An agitated maid came running looking aghast a
the still figure in Richard's arms.

"Miss Lucy?" she squeaked in fright.

"Your eyes play you tricks, girl," he laughed. "Do
you think Miss Lucy has shrunk?"

The sound of voices roused Polly and blinking at her
surroundings she struggled to escape Richard's arms
while the round fiigure of Mrs Carmichael at that
moment came hurriedly down the stairs. Her pink face
was distressed and showed signs of recent tears as she
came towards them.

"Oh, how kind of you to come. I need comfort so
badly."

Fresh tears started to flow and with concern Polly
took her hand while Richard led them to a seat. "Is
something seriously amiss?" he asked and noting a
couple of servants peeping curiously from the kitcher
stairs he called for wine.

"Oh dear, it really is too dreadful and Mr
Carmichael is beside himself. He swears to use his
strongest horsewhip."

Lucy's father appeared without warning, his thin
usually placid face taut, his eyes steely as he looked a
Polly sharply.

"Ah, the girl from Stoke House. What do you know
of this wretched business, miss?"

Bewildered Polly flushed and Richard intervened
"I would appreciate your confidence, sir. Will you
kindly explain what the pother is about? Miss
Wintringham and I have called on an innocent
errand."

Searchingly the farmer looked into their puzzled
faces, then motioning them and his weeping wife to
follow, he stalked away to his study. Polly sank into a
comfortable chair and Richard, uneasy at her fatigued

appearance, stood by her side.

"In spite of your close friendship with my daughter, you were not in her confidence, then?" the man barked swiftly at Polly.

Worriedly she shook her head. "Has something dreadful happened to Lucy?"

Carmichael frowned at his wife's fresh outburst of tears before replying.

"My daughter has seen fit to leave her home and elope with that villain – that – "

Enlightenment dawned on Polly and alert, she sat up. "Hugo! You mean she's run away with Hugo Hamilton?"

"I am very much afraid so. Disgust forbids me mentioning the scoundrel's name, but if I thought you had a hand in it – "

"Oh, no, Mr Carmichael," she answered quickly, striving to keep the pleasure from her face, pleasure at the thought that Lucy, whatever the circumstances, had won her heart's desire.

Richard put an arm about her shoulders. He saw the stupendous shock Lucy had forced on her unhappy parents. Their only child, she was loved and cosseted in spite of her independent ways, and her father had every right to be furious and wounded by her behaviour. But Polly was innocent of any part in the intrigue and he had no intention of seeing her unjustly accused.

"I can understand your predicament, sir," he said quietly, "but, believe me, when I say both Polly and myself are equally astounded by the incident. Neither do I suspect John Hamilton or Arabella of being involved. We have just left Stoke House where Hugo's absence was not remarked upon, possibly because of an equally distressing scene. Polly had hoped to find

asylum with you but it seems an inopportune moment
to trouble you with our problems."

The quivering voice of Mrs Carmichael protested.
She had dried her eyes while endeavouring to gain
control. "Poor little Polly looks completely exhausted.
Do please confide in us, Sir Richard, it might help to
ease our own troubles."

Briefly and as quickly as possible Richard explained
their position while the Carmichaels sat looking
vaguely into space. It was obvious these were both
brooding over Lucy's misdemeanours and not fully
aware of the trials, or indeed the company of the
others.

But when the plump little woman eventually spoke
it was with kindness. "I can see Polly needs rest
immediately and she shall stay here as long as
necessary."

"Thank you," Polly smiled. "But before I take
advantage of your kindness I feel bound in all honesty
to tell you I know of Lucy's affection for Hugo. She has
to my knowledge loved him for months."

"Nonsense!" exploded the girl's father. "I credit my
daughter with greater sense than to moon over such a
ne're-do-well. The Hamilton buck is a cheap
philanderer and I'll never accept him in my house."

"Then you see, Mr Carmichael, why Lucy deceived
you. She guessed your reactions correctly and it
cannot but grieve her."

The farmer's face became purple and reading the
warning sign, Richard ushered the two women
towards the door. He then turned towards the older
man, poured him out a glass of porter, and sat
patiently until the tirade died, an immobile
sympathiser.

Greatly concerned at the rift between Lucy and her parents, Polly did everything in her power to comfort them but when Mrs Carmichael produced the letter announcing Lucy's intention it seemed a difficult task. Asking forgiveness and begging her parents not to completely disown her made Lucy's flight to London with her lover a bewildering contradiction.

"My dear Lucy will never be happy in a bustling city," the unhappy mother lamented, "and I fear her father will never forgive. He talks only of disinheriting her and they were so very compatible."

"I'm sure he will relent but you must wait until the hurt has healed. Hugo's bad reputation is exaggerated, you know, I found him a good friend in adversity."

"You must think me quite heartless and wrapped in my own troubles, my dear. Now tell me of your plans. How soon will you and Sir Richard marry?"

Polly felt this question to be unanswerable. It had been Richard's wish to rush her away to Exeter with a ceremony performed at once, but before agreeing she insisted on knowing how the folk at Stoke House were faring, particularly without Hugo's support. They must by now be aware of the elopement and she hoped such news might penetrate their gloom, for she felt John Hamilton would not be averse to an heiress joining the family.

News was awaited with some anxiety as she hoped to learn Arabella, now resigned, was in a calmer frame of mind. She did not begrudge the unhappy girl the satisfaction of wallowing in misery, neither did she expect her to hide a broken heart; it was quite in character for Arabella to make the most of her ill treatment. Polly imagined the Caldwell girls and others, loud in their condemnation of herself and filled with righteous indignation at the cancellation of such an auspicious wedding.

When Richard returned from Stoke House, however, his face was grave and with a sinking heart Polly met him.

"Arabella is missing," he announced without preamble. "There is no clue to her whereabouts and no one appears aware of her intentions. She may have left the district but the possibility of more serious implications cannot be denied. A search has been organised and, although I may very well be stoned for my pains, the least I can do is to offer help."

Polly assented and begged to assist.

"I think it best for you to stay out of sight at present," he answered. "But I'd feel happier if Hugo could be found. Do you think he might contact that woman you spent a few weeks with last summer?"

"Mrs Lloyd? It's doubtful, she has little time for her country cousins, but surely Mr Hamilton has been in touch with her."

"He failed to remark on it. Do write. No opportunity to trace them must be missed but I wish the Carmichaels were more helpful. They will not or cannot divulge what contacts they have in the City."

"Everything is happening at once, but with all our troubles here I only hope Lucy finds happiness and Hugo proves a better man than everyone gives him credit for."

Richard kept his cynical thoughts to himself, but for Polly's sake, and the unhappy parents, he hoped that a marriage between the runaway couple had already taken place.

Sitting over a neglected supper with the Carmichaels, Polly found even the joy of her new-found love could not remove her depression and a sense of foreboding prevailed. She chafed at her own inactivity and, in spite of Richard's words, was tempted to return to Stoke House. The thought of lonely John Hamilton in need of comfort with Hugo gone and, most frightening of all, Arabella, filled her with dismay.

She stole a glance at the miserable faces of the two elderly people opposite and her eyes filled with tears. She pushed away her plate and rose from the table but a lump in her throat made speech difficult.

"I can't imagine what you think of me for causing such unhappiness." she said, almost inaudibly. "First, Lucy's elopement which, although her own decision, I did my best to encourage, now Arabella's disappearance, which can only be the last straw. I brought it about by my own selfishness, I should have discouraged Richard instead of snatching greedily at his love. I should never have come here to wreck so many lives and I wish my mother's name was still in obscurity. Life could never be so complicated for simple Polly Fielding and even without love people survive.

"How can I marry Richard now when every wave breaking on the shore might cast up Arabella's body. You think she killed herself through my wicked actions, everyone does!"

Her hands gripping the chairback tightly she stood white-faced and the farmer, rising, came towards her. His knowledge of human emotions might be slight but he recognised signs of hysteria, and compassion mingling with shame at his own self-pity stirred him.

Without speaking he led her to the open window, motioning his wife to join them and he looked seriously into the girl's face. When he spoke, if a trifle brusquely, it was not unkindly. "Such stupid nonsense

I never heard tell. Pull yourself together, my girl, remorse never cured an ill, and if guilt torments you, what of Meredith's feelings? His was the promise made to Arabella, his the complete rejection, and he is down on the shore with a conscience, I imagine, killing his every step. To many folk your behaviour is past understanding and only belief in yourselves will weather the storm, but let me tell you this, girl, Arabella's alive somewhere and revelling in all this commotion. She has not the courage to take her own life and revenge is sweet, so they say. Take her punishment without fear, and mark my words, she'll turn up contrite ere long."

For the first time in days she saw the familiar twinkle in his eye and, faltering, Polly looked up. "Thank you for that sensible advice, I don't deserve such kind friends, but Lucy – " she stopped timidly.

The man cleared his throat and looked at his wife and the eagerness in her eyes had him spluttering, "Well, Lucy – we shall see."

Polly's spirits began to rise and when Richard returned weary and depressed she took him into her arms repeating the farmer's words of wisdom. His face relaxed momentarily and she sought for some distraction to keep his fears at bay. It came with startling clarity, for she had, on occasion, thought of the inheritance Arabella now so strangely denied. It might seem mercenary to bring the matter up but if such a mystery diverted Richard from his depression so much the better.

Simply she told him of the expected legacy and he sat up, his eyes alert.

"Am I to marry a clam, then. Why was I not told?"

"I've treated it as of little importance, particularly since Arabella admitted the tale was false, and I'd near forgotten it myself, engrossed in my misery. But Mr Carmichael has taught me the error of my ways and, do you know, I declare before long he'll forgive Lucy and Hugo too."

"I never doubted that, his ranting is but a front, but less provocation, if you please. Tell me more of Arabella's disclosure."

"There's nothing left to tell except I'd hoped to be an heiress and bring you a fine dowry."

He made no further comment but stored the information in the back of his mind. At the moment the problem of Arabella's disappearance must take priority but he had no intention of letting such a peculiar myth escape investigation. He vaguely recalled remarks made by his aunt on Rector Wintringham's wealth that had vanished with his departure from the south. Were it left in trust for Polly, she was surely now of an age to inherit.

Ten

The shops were now full of sprigged muslins and the elaborate frills fast becoming the fashion. Mrs Carmichael insisted Polly shop, for she had very few clothes, her prettiest gowns left behind at Stoke House. Wedding finery must be purchased and stacked away in readiness for the momentous day she became Lady Meredith and mistress of the Manor. The kindly lady declared it now unnecessary to mope about the farm, for Mr Carmichael was well on the way to forgiving his erring daughter and she believed

the slightest move from Lucy could save them all
further sorrow.

A month had passed and the mystery of Arabella
remained unsolved. Ugly rumours circulated in town
and even under Mrs Carmichael's patronage Polly
was openly snubbed by several former friends. It was
glaringly obvious that before her dramatic
disappearance Arabella had informed the whole
county of her betrayal, but with an outwardly
indifferent eye and a firm resolution Polly kept her
dignity.

Richard was impatient for their marriage. He had
come to accept Arabella's absence with calm and
scepticism, feeling they should no longer be subject to
guilt. He had taken to calling regularly at Stoke House
and Polly presumed his sins were forgiven. John
Hamilton needed a familiar face to cheer his lonely
hours and Richard was obviously tolerated, whereas
her own proposed visit was firmly rejected.

Vague on the subject of Hamilton's conduct,
Richard answered her questions tactfully, assuring
her the man seemed under little strain and was
certainly not out of his mind with worry. He agreed
such an attitude was peculiar and privately suspected
the father was shielding the daughter's privacy,
wherever that might be.

With a lighter heart he saw no reason for now
delaying their wedding, but Polly felt loyalty to the
Carmichaels tugging against Richard's demands. She
longed to be his wife, yet hoped to see harmonious
relations restored at the farm before she herself
deserted it. The hope that a letter from Lucy might
reach Stoke House was forlorn, for were it so, the
chances of receiving it were now remote. Richard's
patience finally snapped one day when he appeared at

the farm. Polly was being fitted for an attractive green gown and dainty moroccan slippers with heels to increase her height. Her cheeks were pink at Mrs Carmichael's extravagant compliments and when he burst in upon them, she could not help dimpling at him.

"Polly Wintringham, you are the world's most tantalising creature," he cried in exasperation. "If you refuse to name the day this very minute I swear I'll carry you off to the Manor, marriage or no!"

His voice was full of humour but the grey eyes blazed into her own with desire and she herself knew the time had come. They were unaware that Mrs Carmichael had silently crept away and he covered her face and neck with kisses until she responded with equal ardour.

"Yes, I'll marry you, Richard, whenever you wish, we've waited too long as it is," she cried breathlessly.

"In a week then, and how do you feel about a London wedding? St Bride's perhaps?"

Polly looked thoughtfully at him. Her knowledge of London was slight, with few happy memories, but she guessed a valid reason lay behind his suggestion. The church he suggested sounded very grand, but happily she assented.

"I'd like that very much, but I've no living relatives, you know. I think we must be satisfied with the simplest of ceremonies."

"I've not the slightest doubt the church will be empty and I trust that won't bother you. Has it not struck you, Polly, how few friends we have, you and I?"

"I don't care a fig about that. We have the Carmichaels and Lucy when she reappears with Hugo, but I wish Arabella – "

"I understand your wishes perfectly, darling Polly. Why do you suppose I decided on London for our wedding?"

"To find Lucy and perhaps Arabella. Oh, Richard, I do love you for being so considerate."

"London's a very large place," he laughed, "but one never knows what secrets it hides. It's possible one or two aggravating mysteries might be solved."

Mrs Carmichael shed a few romantic tears when learning of the wedding. "It would have pleased both Mr Carmichael and myself to witness Lucy's nuptials, you know. I long to hear news of her and the young man she loves. Do you think she will be happy, Polly?"

"Most certainly I do and I have a distinct feeling they'll both be back with you before long. You must have known Hugo for years, of course, but perhaps his good points were never appreciated. Very likely Mr Carmichael will soon look upon him as a son."

"That would give me pleasure. I had a son myself, years ago, by my first marriage, you know."

"Lucy told me about that, but he died before she was born, I believe?"

"Yes, he was struck by a runaway horse in Exeter. I never speak of him, in fairness to Mr Carmichael, for it grieves me to think I never gave him a son."

"But Lucy has been a great joy to you."

"Indeed, she has and my husband has never complained. He was acquainted with my son, in fact Theo was the instigation of our meeting, you know."

"Was that his name, Theo?"

The plump lady nodded, her cap ribbons bobbing. "Theodore Spring. He was your grandfather's curate but left the district only months before he was killed."

Polly felt her eyes glazing but kept her voice firm as

she spoke.

"I wish you had told me this earlier."

"But, my dear, it was of no consequence, although I have at times thought your remote connection with my dead son strengthened our affection."

Making no further comment Polly escaped as soon as possible, not trusting her own voice. She discussed the bizarre situation with an astounded Richard.

"It seems ludicrous that she is my grandmother and Lucy my aunt. What shall I do? Have I the right to betray the forgotten lovers? Surely producing the intimate letters would serve no good purpose now?"

He was thoughtful for a while then answered her sagely. "The decision must be entirely yours, my dear, but, personally, I cannot see the relevance. Indeed, such a shock might damage the happy relationship existing between man and wife. Their mutual regard is enhanced at present by their concern for Lucy and I feel no further worries should burden them. Whether you reveal all to Lucy one day is your own affair, but she seems a sensible girl and well able to use her discretion."

"Perhaps you are right. But do you know, Richard, the death of Theo troubles me. That accident might well have been his own doing. We have no right to judge of course, but I can never think well of him."

"Caroline Mary Wintringham, I find your family complications more trying every minute and the sooner your name is changed to Meredith the happier I shall be!"

They were married the following week in London. Polly tactfully avoided the fussy pink gown Mrs Carmichael admired and the simple cream silk she chose gave her skin a warm glow. Her red hair shone unadorned and with Richard resplendent in claret-coloured broadcloth they complemented each other admirably.

Lack of a congregation was scarcely noticed but the Carmichaels hot and uncomfortable in city finery, seemed daunted by the lofty church and as they left neither Polly nor Richard could help seeing how eagerly their eyes scanned the crowded streets, searching hopelessly, as Richard later remarked, for Lucy to appear as if by magic.

Their lodging house in St James's was elegant and frequented by high-born gentlemen and ladies of distinction. Polly's eyes flashed with amusement at some of their antics, but for all their affectations, none in her eyes could compare with Richard.

They visited Vauxhall Gardens and the play at Drury Lane and Polly discovered the sound of great music in the Opera House.

It was when they were leaving that hall of fame that Mrs Frances Lloyd was encountered. That popular hostess bowed graciously to Polly before peering at Sir Richard with her quizzing-glass, whereupon she beamed with delight.

"How well met, Miss Fielding, I trust you found the opera entertaining."

"Oh, yes, indeed, Mrs Lloyd." Polly bowed slightly and gently pressed Richard's arm. "But I must beg you no longer call me Miss Fielding, may I present my husband, Sir Richard Meredith?"

The lady weighed Richard up shrewdly before digging him heartily in the ribs. "I never thought you'd be trapped, my boy, by a minx clever enough to outwit Arabella."

Looking from one to the other Polly felt nonplussed. "Do you know each other?" she asked with a puzzled frown.

"Of course we do, you foolish child, you have to learn much of your new husband, I suspect. Not that he comes to town often enough, burying himself in that God-forsaken county! However, you must now persuade him into a London season." She suddenly gave a delighted laugh. "I must say life has dealt you many surprises since leaving my house, my dear. As for you, sir," she turned to Richard beaming, "you've shown excellent taste in a bride. This child is a raving beauty, set on taking London by storm and worth two of my disagreeable niece.

Polly coloured furiously and faltered. "You've heard the tale, I suppose, and how worried we are about Arabella. Is there a chance you might have seen her, Mrs Lloyd?"

"None whatever and, if you ask me, that devious brother of mine has a finger in this unsavoury pie. But do not distress yourself, life is too short. A soirée is about to start at my house and so romantic a couple is more than welcome. Please do attend."

Polly shrank away but Richard, his hand firmly on her arm, bowed with a charming smile and accepted. He begged an hour's grace and when they were alone spoke soothingly. "I never imagined you a shrinking violet, Polly. I know from past experience how you love to dance, so why so reluctant tonight?"

"Well, you see," she answered hesitantly, "I might possibly have served some of Mrs Lloyd's guests before. I'd be so humiliated if I were recognised as the former lady's maid."

"I'll swear you never will be. You shall wear your prettiest gown and mingle with princes, hold your head high, my dearest Polly, and you could pass as a princess yourself. How much more fitting than those pathetic creatures in the royal household."

"You really do dispel my gloom," she laughed.
"But it surprised me to find you so friendly with Mrs
Lloyd. When she was mentioned a while ago you
didn't speak of her."

"My dear Polly, if I spoke of every passing
acquaintance your head would simply whirl."

"I'm sure it would, but I'm determined to enjoy the
party. Do you realise we might even hear news of
Arabella?"

"Exactly what I was thinking myself," he answered
smoothly.

"Richard!" She stared in surprise at his grinning
face. "I do believe you purposely inveigled that
invitation."

"Well, do remember," came the bland reply,
"although Arabella is not popular with her aunt, very
likely Hugo is."

Polly's heart quickened. "Hugo and Lucy – can she
know of the elopement?"

"It's more than possible. If only one of our problems
can be solved, what better it were done in entertaining
company?"

The popularity of Frances Lloyd's soirée was
evident, for a smart, well-dressed set gathered at her
house. Music and laughter under blazing chandeliers,
with wine and exotic food never before tasted, kept
Polly's eyes wide with wonder and Richard grinning
appreciatively at her. He bade her take note of
amusing novelties, for the time was approaching when
she herself must act as hostess. She smiled a little
ruefully at his enthusiasm, wondering apprehensively
if anyone in the county would enter the portals of the
house of such a scandalous couple as they. But
Richard was full of assurance. "Don't fret about such
things, memories are conveniently short at times and

many will fidget to appraise the Manor's new mistress."

"But I object to people coming simply to satisfy their curiosity, I want to welcome them as friends."

"So you shall, my dearest Polly. Just have a little patience."

She smiled up into his confident face, her heart near bursting with pride. He was without doubt the handsomest man in the room, in his faultless attire, his thick hair shining and his grey eyes gleaming with love for her alone. Surprised by the number of people acknowledging him with familiarity she was fast becoming aware of his distinction. The life of the country squire she had married evidently stretched a good deal further than Devon and she realised the demanding life of town might very often claim them.

Later, as they swept in unison with a line of dancers, they both saw a sight to astound them, for standing close in heated discussion were Hugo Hamilton and his father.

As soon as it was possible they retired from the cotillion and Richard hurried Polly away. She was shaking with excitement.

"If Hugo is here, Lucy must be, too. Oh, Richard, how wonderful."

Tactfully he steered her from the lobby where they stood and into a small sitting-room.

"They were too engrossed to notice us, I believe. I want you to stay here, Polly, while I discover what's afoot."

"Oh, no, Richard, please let me be with you, I must discover where Lucy is."

"You shall do so later. Hugo's presence is not surprising but that of Hamilton is, particularly as Mrs Lloyd professes little love is lost between them. I refuse

to have you involved, darling, but I promise not to
leave you alone for long. Allow me just ten minutes."

Unwillingly she was forced to agree and she
wandered restlessly about the room. Many irritating
things scratched at her mind. Was Mrs Lloyd, in spite
of her protestations, deceiving them? Had she
knowledge of Arabella, and did she intend to
deliberately mislead them? And yet with what
enthusiasm they were received in her home, and how
generous were her praises.

Slowly the minutes passed while she awaited
Richard's return, and frequently she glanced at the
firmly closed door. When, her patience almost
exhausted, it eventually opened, she flew across the
room but was unprepared for the figure standing in
the doorway.

Stylishly dressed, her face in its radiance almost
beautiful, and laughing with pleasure, stood Lucy.
She held her arms wide and with muffled greetings
they clung to each other joyfully.

Polly's heart felt fit to burst with happiness as with
Richard she walked in the garden of a small but pretty
house on the outskirts of town.

"I can't believe everything is falling into place so
beautifully and I do believe Hugo has changed beyond
recognition. He seems exceptionally fond of Lucy and
I'm sure they are happy together."

"I'm inclined to agree, they appear ideally suited,
for I fancy she'll stand no nonsense from him. How
long he'll be content to live in these surroundings
remains to be seen."

"But it's such a sweet little house. Oh, I wish the
Carmichaels had not rushed so hastily back to Devon.
They couldn't fail to be pleased about Lucy's

happiness."

"I've given that matter some thought and, in my opinion, they're entitled to a little information. I've not forgotten their understanding of our problems and would like to repay it, but I feel a formal letter to be inadequate."

"Lucy would probably object to your interference."

"Very likely, but for all that I've a mind to go back to Devon myself and put the true facts before them."

Polly clapped her hands. "What an excellent idea and perhaps I could stay here with Lucy until you return, we have so much to discuss together."

"Does that mean the minx is prepared to happily let me go? Can you bear to spend a week without a husband who is desolate at an hour apart?"

"Oh, stupid! Of course I'll miss you, and I'll only allow an absence of four days. Tell the Carmichaels of Lucy's blooming and how well Hugo is providing for them both. He's refused to touch a penny of her money, you know."

He thought her eyes had never looked so brilliant as they shone with enthusiasm and the words bubbled joyfully from her. "I've never felt so happy in my life. All we need now is Arabella's return – are you sure Mr Hamilton knows where she's hiding?"

As he left her with assurances, Polly sat on a little rustic seat where the sun filtered through the sapling trees. She recalled last night's reunion with Lucy as between happy tears they learned of each other's bliss. There was so much to say, so much to discover, that the elegant soirée was forsaken and Hugo insisted on driving them back to the tiny residence he and Lucy had purchased.

Here they talked far into the night, she and Lucy ecstatic, Richard and Hugo surprisingly compatible.

It appeared that until arriving at his aunt's house for the ball, Hugo was unaware of the mystery of Arabella. Whether Mrs Lloyd knew the facts and intended keeping them from him was uncertain, he said, but his father's unexpected appearance greatly surprised and annoyed his aunt, as indeed it did Hugo himself.

"But what is your father doing in London?" Polly asked. "Is he on the trail of Arabella?"

Hugo looked at Richard, who nodded, and they pieced together all that was known.

Hamilton had told them that Arabella was temporarily residing in the city, that he knew of her address but would give no reason for his intrusion at the ball.

"But Arabella is perfectly well and has recovered her senses?" Polly had anxiously asked.

"According to Papa, greatly improved," she was answered with a grin. "You should be aware that my sister's a sight too high and mighty for her own good. I'll wager she heaped coals of fire unmercifully on your guilty heads."

Ruefully they had agreed, then Lucy in the peace of her own house enquired quietly about her parents. She was pathetically eager to learn about Polly's stay on the farm and the details of their wedding, her eyes aglow with affectionate interest. Polly knew when the opportunity arose she would have no hesitation in revealing to this girl, already loved like a sister, their true relationship.

When at dinner that day, Richard suggested that Polly stay for a few days while he left town on business, Lucy looked extremely thoughtful.

"Where exactly does your business take you, Richard?" she asked innocently.

Hugo, astute, but never the most tactful of fellows, burst into laughter. "You've only to look at the guilt on his face to learn he's off on a jaunt to Devon."

Richard frowned but Lucy was quietly insistent. "Is that so, Richard, horse-trading, I presume?"

"Something like that," he nodded.

With a flaming face Polly's bent head failed to hide her discomfort and the other girl raised an eyebrow before speaking without expression. "If you have other business in Devon, I trust it does not concern my affairs, Richard. I refuse to let anyone interfere with my private life."

"Come, my love," Hugo protested, but apart from a fond look she ignored him.

"Oh, Lucy, we were hoping to plead your case," Polly cried, "your poor parents have no means of contact, but we believe they would welcome the slightest sign – "

"Exactly, a personal sign from me." Lucy paused looking around the table and Polly saw the placid unperturbed Lucy was tremulous. When she spoke again her voice was low. "I suppose I should have previously discussed this decision with my husband, forgive me, darling Hugo. But I believe the time has now come to contact my family and although not for a moment regretting my actions, I feel perhaps I was harsh on them. I must confess I feel homesick, not only to see their faces, but also for the sea and the sweet country air. If you insist on returning to Devon, Richard, will you allow me to join you?"

"Do you think I would let you go alone, by Gad, to face them without my support?" Hugo cried.

"No, I don't think you would." Tears stood in the indomitable Lucy's eyes and Hugo rose and went towards her.

"I'll go with you quite happily and together we'll try a reconciliation. Heaven knows it's where we belong and London may keep its pleasure. By God, the city bores me at times!"

Polly could scarcely believe Hugo's congeniality and cried with her heart racing. "Oh, yes, let us all go home, Richard, if you please."

Her husband's face showed relief and pleasure as he answered heartily, "We'll leave in the morning, if everyone agrees."

Suddenly Polly's face clouded. "But I forgot Mr Hamilton and Arabella. What can we do about them?"

"A fig to them," Richard answered firmly. "We've wasted enough time on Arabella. She has her own life and I've no doubt she'll enjoy it without interference. We owe nothing more to either of them."

Eleven

Although to Polly's knowledge no forewarning was given, she found on their arrival at the Manor a small army of servants awaiting in the hall. It took all her courage to face them but as Richard led her through the ranks she gained confidence from his self-assurance and, ignoring the curious stares, she swept up the grand staircase with formal dignity.

Grinning with delight her husband praised her performance but was unaware with what misgivings the numerous corridors and unexpected rooms were viewed. She felt full of apprehension as Richard strolled unconcernedly along, apparently filled with confidence in the capabilities he fancied she possessed.

"Oh dear, I feel quite overwhelmed at such spaciousness," she murmured worriedly, "and I can't help but envy Lucy's unimposing London house. I fear I shall make the most hideous mistakes and I do hope my inexperience won't disappoint you, Richard."

"Do I appear so inconsiderate? I have every confidence in you, darling Polly, and all I wish is your happiness. It is perhaps fortunate that you see the house at its best with, spring as a recommendation. Every room in our apartments has a view of the sea, which, as a mermaid I'm sure you'll appreciate, but when winter comes and the coast is bleak, the place whistles with devilish winds. We'll find a comfortable house in London then, as tiny and cosy as you wish."

Before she could reply he paused before a door she found quite familiar, and with a conspiratorial look and a flourish he flung it wide open. Before her stretched Regina's vacated room bearing little resemblance to the former stuffy overfilled atmosphere. Now delicate painted furniture rested tastefully on a pastel carpet and exquisite little treasures enticed her inside. The smell of fresh flowers displayed in profusion brought a cry of delight and through the open window where dainty muslin fluttered in the breeze, a glimpse of the sea, sparkling like jewels in the summer sunshine, entranced her.

Words seemed inadequate as she turned to Richard with starry eyes and he gathered her tenderly into his arms.

"There are other rooms in our suite which I hope will please you, but nothing equals the beauty of your eyes," he muttered thickly against her hair. She slipped from his grasp teasingly. "Tell me now about the rest of the house.''

"Only if you stay on my knee! Later you shall see what work must be done to restore former glory. A great deal of damage has been done by neglect, but I've no doubt a transformation will eventually take place. We have the rest of our lives to achieve it.''

"I'd never want to see the tradition lost of which you are so proud.''

They were allowed little time to plan their immediate future, for Lucy occupied much of Polly's mind and with impatience news from the farm was awaited.

Within two days, however, an answer in the form of a carriage arrived. Richard was down at the stables, but Polly, a basket of flowers on her 'arm, came running from the garden to see a radiant figure alight.

"Everything has slipped beautifully into place,'' Lucy cried reassuringly, "and how I blame myself for my stubborn pride.'' She slipped her arm through Polly's and smiled into the eager face. "I'm not strictly a sentimental person, as you know, but I think we were all emotionally affected and Mama is still prone to happy tears! I have never seen Papa so moved – '' Her eyes moist, she blew her nose, and quickly Polly enquired, "Was Hugo cordially received?''

"Quite amiably, if not with over-enthusiasm. But our thoughtless conduct is already forgiven, and they are prepared to give Hugo a chance to prove his worth. They realise if he is unacceptable I shall be too, and somehow I feel none of us wants further discord.''

"What wonderful news, I'm so relieved, and your parents must be quite overjoyed by it all. Now tell me about your plans.''

"We shall stay at the farm for a few weeks until we find a house of our own. Hugo is determined to be independent of Papa, but I feel he might ask Richard's advice about breeding. Such a way of life would suit us perfectly, after all I am not inexperienced myself with horses and we may very well establish a successful stud."

"What a splendid idea, I'm sure Richard will be eager to help. But do come into the house, I've so much to show you."

Together they wandered through the renovated rooms, and Lucy, remembering the dark forbidding Manor as a child, enthused at the transformation. The affectionate bond, always prevalent between them, blossomed as they sat drinking tea, and on a sudden impulse Polly revealed their new-found relationship. Astounded, Lucy could scarcely credit such coincidence, but together they hugged their secret, both agreeing so personal a thing should be kept confidential, even to the exclusion of Lucy's mother – principally to preserve her peace of mind. Explaining her own mother's letters, Polly admitted Richard's involvement and Lucy with perfect understanding, accepted this.

Lucy refused an invitation to dinner, for Hugo, now at Stoke House for the purpose of collecting his personal belongings, was expecting her to join him.

Polly, feeling a sentimental urge to see the white stone house where once many happy hours were spent, suggested they drove over with Lucy, and Richard raised no objection to this, since because Hamilton was absent the moment seemed opportune.

Before the matter could be decided, however, an interruption came in the shape of Oliver, arriving on a frisky new mare. He dismounted breezily before them, grown in six months to a lanky confident schoolboy and Polly knew an affectionate demonstration would only cause embarrassment. He grinned cheerfully at them, airily declaring, "If Hugo thinks I'm still his whipping-boy, he's very much mistaken, but as there's little for me to do, and you are so newly wed, Lucy, I thought I'd grant him this favour."

Lucy laughed and bobbed a playful curtsy, "Honoured, I'm sure, sir. Pray tell me my master's bidding."

"Oh, fie, Lucy! I'll wager you'll never bow to Hugo. But I'm sent with instructions to escort you to Stoke House." He paused frowning thoughtfully. "I think all of you should come, Arabella's home."

The laughter around him suddenly died, and Richard asked quickly, "Is your father with her?"

"Yes," the boy nodded. "They arrived last night, some hours after I did – it's school holiday, you know."

Polly looked at Richard for guidance, considering now the inexpediency of visiting Stoke House with Arabella in residence. If, as she hoped, normality was returning there, she had no wish to stir up further conflict.

"There's no need to be so bashful," Oliver scoffed nonchalantly, "I know all about both marriages, the whole town is buzzing with news, and as part of the family I think it uncommonly mean that nobody wrote me about it."

"It all happened quite suddenly – " Lucy began.

"I know. Well, I'll forgive you and I must say what a lark it is having you for a sister. I'm sure you'll not fuss, like Arabella does."

Richard was contemplating. "If all is well with the family, I see no reason for Polly and I to come along. Will you be good enough to escort Lucy alone, Oliver."

"Oh, no, sir. Hugo insisted I bring you all. Besides,

Arabella is chirpy, she has a new beau to boast of."

Three pairs of surprised eyes surveyed the boy.
Polly's bright with relief and satisfaction, Lucy's a
little cynical and Richard's full of amusement as he
turned to order the carriage.

As they bowled along in the warm sunshine the two
girls gossiped reflectively on Oliver's unsatisfactory
description of the newcomer. They gathered he was
important and wealthy, and in the boy's words —
decidedly elderly.

As they drew rein before the house, Polly felt her
throat tighten with nerves. Her last meeting with
Arabella was still vividly clear, the bitter hurt of her
angry words not yet forgotten, but Lucy's smile of
encouragement and the confident squeeze of her hand
did much to restore her confidence.

Hugo was on the steps and in the bright sunlit hall,
familiar and warm, stood John Hamilton, a welcome
smile on his face. Gallantly he praised both girls'
appearance, enquiring of their health and calling for
wine in much the same breath. Stimulated, he was
obviously in the highest spirits, with not a whit of
embarrassment.

Confused, Polly warily watched the man's
unpredictable behaviour, but she met him with
outward calm, and Richard's eyes meeting hers with
approval boosted her confidence.

"How pleasant to find my house filled with youthful
vitality once more, a gathering of old friends cannot be
surpassed," Hamilton enthused. "Kindly inform
Arabella we have company, Oliver. I am sure our
young friends will be anxious to meet her future
husband."

"Is Arabella to be married soon?" Polly asked in a
fluster of surprise while Lucy raised her eyebrows

significantly.

Hamilton nodded knowingly as Richard enquired:
"Not a local man, I presume?"

"Indeed, no, they met in London three weeks ago
and I feel she has done very well for herself considering
her past misfortune." He coughed discreetly,
"However, such unpleasantness is in the past and my
daughter is to wed an earl, no less."

"An honour indeed," Hugo, who had been sullenly
silent, exploded disagreeably and Lucy laid a
restraining hand on his arm.

At that moment a stranger, middle-aged and
sturdy, breezed into the house. His riding-boots were
splashed with sea-spray, Polly suspected, and his face,
although florid, glowed with good nature. If this was
the earl, he seemed affable enough and she glanced at
Richard approvingly.

"A perfect day for a canter," the fellow enthused,
"and the whole of England has no better coastline. I'd
forgotten the pleasures of it, Hamilton."

"I barely expected you back so soon, best get out of
those damp breeches at once."

"The devil take it, John, you're becoming a regular
shrew. Do your duty, man, and present me to the
ladies. I never could resist a pretty face, you know."

Suddenly Richard laughed and at his first words
Polly knew she was mistaken in thinking this man the
earl.

"I remember you well, sir," he said with pleasure.
"Did you not deal with my father's estate some years
ago, my name is Meredith."

"Well, so it is – you have a good memory for faces,
young man, but so have I, even though you were but a
stripling when last we met." He held out his hand and
clasped Richard's firmly. "Henry Burrow's my name,

former partner to John Hamilton, and well I recall your father, God save his soul. I hear your aunt has now gone to rest."

Richard nodded briefly. "It must be years since you visited Devon."

"A sight too many, and I welcome the business that brought my return."

The man paused, looking searchingly at Polly, who stood holding Richard's arm. "There's little need to present this young lady, Caroline Mary Wintringham, I presume?"

Polly found her hands clasped in two very large ones. "I'd know you anywhere, my dear, the image of your mother," he said.

"Really?" With eagerness her heart soared as she looked up into his kindly face and impulsively she cried, "I can never learn enough about her, Mr Borrow, do tell – "

Instinct told her Hamilton's face was dark with disapproval and she paused, at the same moment meeting with relief Arabella appearing on the stairs.

In her slow, slightly ponderous way, the girl descended, her hand resting lightly on the arm of a faultlessly dressed little man. Either he still resorted to powder or his hair was liberally sprinkled with grey, but his advanced years were soon apparent to all the young people. His face had an ivory pallor, the aquiline nose held high but there seemed not a surplus ounce of flesh on his small, sprightly body. Arabella looked much as usual, a little plump but serene, and almost beautiful in a pompous kind of way.

Her father went forward and with visible satisfaction took the girl's hand. "What homage, Arabella," he beamed, "Hugo is home with his new bride and Richard and Polly are here bringing felicitations.''

His daughter's dark eyes did not flicker as she kissed the girls and gave her hand to the two men, then turning to the one by her side, no taller than her shoulder, she presented her future husband, Roderick, Earl of Marcelon.

With introductions over, the party mingled in a more relaxed mood and everyone carefully avoided reference to the past troubled weeks, while Arabella, already adopting the part of a gracious lady, discussed plans for her grand wedding, to take place within a month.

Round-eyed with disbelief, Polly's eyes met those of Lucy, whose sparkled with wicked amusement, and over congratulatory toasts she looked round for the interesting Mr Borrow. The possibility of a word with him at the moment seemed very remote.

"I do hope he doesn't leave the district before we can talk about my mother,'' she confided to Richard as soon as etiquette permitted their departure. "As Mr Hamilton's previous partner he must know a great deal about her. He seems very fond of the country, I wonder why he left to live in town.''

"Circumstances, I expect, although his sudden return after all these years is interesting. Surely, though, Polly, there is little left to know of your own background.''

She sat silently brooding, then shook her head humorously. "Perhaps you are right and I'm fanciful, but Mr Borrow impressed me, he looks so dependable.''

In spite of relief and a certain pleasure that Arabella had reappeared in no whit perturbed, Polly could see by Richard's frown how vexed he was by the girl's cool conduct, and hastily she remarked, "It seems scarcely credible that a few weeks ago we all despaired of Arabella. I'm still confused at her behaviour. Do you think she's been staying at Lord Marcelon's London house?"

"Unlikely, I'd say, although possibly they have mutual friends. Personally, I consider her actions extremely irresponsible and quite premeditated."

"Well, it does seem possible her father knew all along of her whereabouts."

"I'd stake my favourite filly on that and he's led us a pretty dance. Obviously, it was his intention to make us suffer and it must have been a tremendous shock to discover us at the soirée."

"A shock for us too, you remember. I suppose he was in town on account of Arabella's betrothal."

"So I imagine, but he put in an appearance at Mrs Lloyd's – much I am sure to that lady's annoyance – in the hope of finding Hugo."

"Well, somehow I feel everything is nicely concluded," Polly said with a sigh of relief.

Their eyes met, hers thoughtful but his satirical as he teased, "Does the earl have any appeal for you?"

"None at all, he must be dreadfully old, but, I suspect, considerably wealthy."

"Rich enough to please the prospective bride and her father, I'm sure."

"Poor Arabella. It's difficult to believe she'll find happiness with such a dull fellow and I must confess to feeling guilty even now at stealing her handsome lover."

He hugged her to him. "Nonsense, the prize she has captured is more fitting for her ego. The seats of Marcelon are famed for their luxury and I've no doubt her name will soon be familiar in William's respectable court. All the Queen's ladies resemble

Arabella, she will fit in very neatly and with the utmost satisfaction."

"What a comfort you are, you make me feel so cherished but also insufferably smug, and I suppose you are right about Arabella, at least my conscience simply longs to agree."

Suddenly the brilliant light of summer shone over the little town and the word that Arabella was to wed an English earl spread like wildfire.

A local wedding was decided upon, for the bridegroom, in spite of his frigid appearance, was inclined to indulge his young intended and happily comply with her wishes. It surprised everyone to find him a bachelor, for the public expected so distinguished a man of his years to be surrounded by sons. His single state gratified Arabella, however, and she had every intention of producing the heirs expected of her.

That gentleman returned to London to prepare his town house for the bride, leaving behind a great bustle at Stoke House. Preparations for a wedding far exceeding in importance the aborted one kept the household in frenzied activity.

Polly was surprised at her old friend's affability and it was obvious others had been warned to treat her with similar consideration. The absence of slights and snubs was noticeable: indeed, the Caldwell girls and others were so overawed by the trio of such stupendous events that an air of restraint prevailed. They gathered around Arabella like adoring subjects and she behaved in much the same way a condescending queen would.

She begged Polly and Lucy, as new brides, to advise her on important details, and many private confidences were exchanged. Richard was highly amused by the situation, teasing Polly for her participation, but pleased to see gone the pinched look of anxiety she had previously worn. She glowed with a happiness he shrank from diminishing, but suspicion of John Hamilton persisted and the defrauding of his wife, which he now seriously considered, could not be tolerated. He felt the only person capable of enlightening him on the subject was Henry Borrow, and as this gentleman agreed to extend his visit until after the wedding, a private discussion should not prove difficult.

A small supper party to include that gentleman was arranged with Mr and Mrs Carmichael, Hugo and Lucy as the other guests. Richard looked at his radiant wife across the table with pride and abounding love. She had bowed to fashion and wore an absurd little feathered concoction in her hair which danced with her vivacious movements. He half listened to the chatter as quiet servants served delicious food and it seemed incredible that this lofty room, now sparkling with handsome silver, had once been swathed in gloom. That fortune was smiling on him and his friends brought a feeling of utter contentment and he felt entitled to a little complacency.

The company were discussing a property that Lucy had found on the lower cliff. Once a pleasant house, it was now neglected and lonely, but sheltered by rocks it escaped the buffeting winds and there was every possibility of making it into a charming refuge. The present state of repair was unimportant, Lucy declared, and she sought Mr Borrow's expert advice.

Hugo was slightly cynical about his wife's enthusiasm for the house but was glad enough to leave domestic arrangements to her, for his time was taken in looking for good bloodstock, with Richard's valuable aid.

"My wife has a habit of convincing everyone black is white," he laughed. "She's a witch at bullying folk, sir, I'm giving you fair warning."

"She has a very sensible approach, if I may say so, young man, and I'll look at the property tomorrow." The genial man turned to Mr Carmichael. Your daughter's brain is acute, sir, you must be extremely proud of her in these days of flibbertigibbets."

The farmer nodded gravely, while eyeing Lucy with affection.

"Old property has many attributes," Borrow continued. "I rode to the old Rectory this morning and was dismayed to discover its ruinous condition. Does it not distress you, Lady Meredith, to find your mother's home so derelict?"

Polly smiled mistily. "There are reasons to be grateful for its sorry state, but, naturally, I would consider renovation were it possible."

"Better by far to demolish the lot and build a folly there if you must."

As Polly sought Richard's eyes he nodded slightly and she felt that indeed her cup of happiness was full.

Twelve

With supper over, Richard noticed Henry Borrow's critical eye appraising the Manor and suggested a tour of the house. It must be many years since his elderly guest had set foot here and an expert's opinion on the renovated gallery would give him satisfaction.

The leisurely manner in which they strolled did little to curb his impatience, but at last, on reaching his study, Richard steered Borrow skilfully to the privacy inside. With sturdy legs stretched comfortably before him, guest looked at host over a glass of port, a beaming countenance masking the shrewdness in his eyes.

" 'Pon my soul this is a pleasure, my boy, the house has more life than I recollect and I see naught but smooth sailing. But I doubt you ensnared me for nothing, suppose you come to the point."

"Is it so obvious?" came the rueful reply.

"Perfectly, if I may say so. When not behaving like a cat full of cream you've been fidgeting most of the evening. As there seems to be little amiss with the property, instinct tells me the problem concerns your new wife."

"You are more than observant, sir, and indeed Polly's welfare is much on my mind. While a breach of professional etiquette is not expected, a word on the subject of her grandfather would be appreciated."

Receiving a nod of encouragement he continued.

"Before my Aunt Regina died she hinted at Rector Wintringham's considerable wealth. She may have been under a misapprehension, on the other hand, were such rumours true, the possibility of Polly being an heiress must be considered."

"What gives you the impression it is any concern of mine?"

"I understand when his daughter died, the Rector left the district, were you not then a partner of John Hamilton's?"

"True, but that was years ago. I'm simply a visitor now. Surely Hamilton can answer your queries, you've known each other for years."

"The matter is not as simple as that, sir, will you do me the honour of listening to my tale?"

Quietly and without emotion, Richard explained Arabella's indiscretion regarding the inheritance. "You probably knew at that time of the Rector's intention to abandon Polly."

"Yes, I was aware of it. Wintringham went off to Norfolk alone and the babe was wet-nursed by a farmer's wife until that good lady died."

"So I understand. I wonder the Godly fellow stopped at murdering the child. How much more convenient had she died with her mother!" came the savage reply.

"Your anger is understandable, he was a hard man, but he christened the child before leaving, as the parish register proves. As time passed he placed a headstone on his daughter's grave, it was a kind of atonement."

"A charming gesture, I'm sure. But it's difficult to believe Hamilton's benevolence received no compensation. It occurs to me the Rector's gold was likely to be left in trust and as Polly's guardian

Hamilton would have complete monopoly. Strange don't you think?''

"That sounds like an accusation. Do you suspect him of stealing her birthright?''

His question remained unanswered and in the silent room Borrow studied the face opposite his. He saw the firm jaw stubbornly set, the eyes full of purpose, but he also saw a man to be envied, wanting for nothing, the world at his feet, and thoughtfully he asked;

"Is the issue of such importance to you?''

"For my wife's sake it certainly is. Neither you nor I, sir, have known the ignoble sin of poverty, but consider a girl like Polly, fresh and sweet and eternally grateful to those she considered her betters. Was such subservience really necessary?''

He raised his hand at the other, about to interrupt. "Please hear me out, sir. The Rector was undoubtedly the harsh man you describe, insisting his grand-daughter be kept ignorant of her birth. He obviously dreaded the inheritance of her mother's shocking sins, but I cannot believe his pride would allow her to live for ever on charity, nor would he wish another to blatantly rob her. Forgive me for involving you in such a distasteful affair, but your partnership was dissolved at that time and I feel perhaps you, too, harboured grave suspicions.''

"My own feelings, in all sincerity, cannot be disclosed, but I shall not deny there was some speculation at the time, although my own participation in the case was negligible. But you surely don't expect me to betray another man's secrets? Hamilton is a trustworthy friend with a reputation beyond reproach and I feel, young man, no good will come of stirring up the past.''

"You think not?'' came the grim remark. "I see we

differ considerably there and if I discover Hamilton to
be the fraud I suspect, every court in Devon shall learn
of his trickery.''

In the luxurious room Polly stood her hair loose about
her shoulders, the flimsy bedgown outlining her figure
as soft breezes blew from an open window. Richard
thought she had never looked lovelier and longed to
crush her in his arms, but the anger at what he
considered Hamilton's treachery eclipsed all else.

"It cannot be true," she cried aghast. "He would
never willingly deceive me, he was always so
considerate —''

"Naturally, it suited his purpose.'' The curt voice
answering might have been a stranger's. "Your
schooldays have little importance, a duty considered
appropriate no doubt, but bringing you to Stoke
House as companion to Arabella — little more than a
servant — *that* I'll never forgive.

"And Hugo, how convenient for him to find a girl
ignorant of her worth, it must have caused
consternation when you refused his advances and they
saw what was left of your money slipping away!''

She stood transfixed, remembering voices overheard
on a summer's night.

"Hugo had no conception of such a thing and
neither had Arabella, I'm sure.''

"But her later confidence was not so absurd after
all, it was foolish of us to ignore it. I feel you are over-
gullible, Polly, but it might interest you to know I've
long mistrusted Hamilton.''

Polly gazed at this unknown man snapping at her so
balefully and her nervousness gave way to annoyance.
"Was that considered too trivial for my ears or did you
fear I might dismiss such a ridiculous notion?''

His eyes were dark as he turned away and she pleaded. "Does it matter now, Richard? I have all I want in the world, others are unimportant and I am perfectly content – "

"Perhaps you are, by Gad, but I've no intention of letting this pass! It might be a little late for recompense but I intend making Hamilton sweat for every minute you slaved in that damned school, for every single penny of your grandfather's money he spent on God knows what! And if he cannot produce what is rightfully yours it will give me pleasure to see him hauled off to jail."

"Oh, Richard, no! Please be a little more tolerant, he was honest enough to educate me."

"Was he, Polly? How honest was accepting your servitude over the years, how honest that every meal you ate was repaid in some chore? It was your right to be treated with homage and dressed in the silk Arabella wore. Very likely her finery was purchased with your own gold."

"I really think your attitude extraordinary, Richard, and your accusations almost certainly false. What positive proof have you of a legacy? Mr Borrow gave you none."

She sank into a chair while he strode about the room, vowing vengeance, too infurated to notice her distress as, near to tears, she continued: "To accuse Arabella's father after all these years is scandalous and can't you see the ruination of her wedding plans?"

"Are you trying to tell me you condone such behaviour, that Hamilton should be excused?"

"Not necessarily, but I wonder how Lord Marcelon will react. Do please consider, Richard – "

"My consideration is only for you and the indignities you've suffered. You cannot prevent me from seeing justice done."

The hot eyes before her made Polly's cool by comparison and her voice now controlled was firm. "I feel this is my affair and although you are my husband please don't interfere. *I* shall decide if I think it necessary what action to take against John Hamilton."

He stared in disbelief before smiling as he came towards her.

"While admiring your spirit, darling, I feel your conduct quite irresponsible. Stop behaving like a tiresome child."

She slipped from his hands, answering tartly. "There's nothing I dislike more than being called a child, but I can behave as wilfully as one. It is not my intention to cause a furore over this matter and if you insist on chastising Mr Hamilton, do so by all means, but only when I permit."

Her eyes were blazing into his while uncontrollable words poured forth. "You seem so incensed with this business that I wonder at your concern. Is it entirely on my behalf or does the gold have greater importance? I've heard that great wealth makes people avaricious, am I to believe this of you?"

Savagely his hand closed on her wrist and he drew her towards him. "Do you really believe me so contemptible that I'd stoop to such lengths for my own ends?"

His voice was bitter and he released her so abruptly she staggered.

"You must learn more of my ways, my dear, and show a little discretion. Surely you realise how greatly I resent taking orders, particularly from a woman. I have always done exactly as I pleased and without your permission shall continue to do so."

As he left, Polly sank trembling on to the bed. She felt sick and ashamed of her absurd accusations. That they were made in an attempt to prevent him bringing fraudulent charges against Hamilton, he would never believe, but should he persevere with such foolish intentions the success of their marriage must be at stake. How could they bear to face each other with the unmistakable taint of money between them.

Slowly she dressed and went down to the stables, where the lovely little filly now her own neighed a sleepy welcome. There was no denying Richard would make Stoke House his destination and, torn between joining him and hiding away in her misery, she rode aimlessly into the moonlit night. Her heart was heavy for the man she loved better than life, and the sudden rift blown between them.

Without purpose she cantered over the heath until the sound of another horse was heard and turning she saw it approaching.

"Why, Mr Borrow, what an unexpected meeting."

"True, my dear, and your solitary state astounds me. Is your husband so careless to allow you licence at this hour?"

The kind bantering words found her colouring, and turning away she made an effort to appear cool.

"Richard is about, we often ride at night, but I suspect he's on the beach."

"I spied a fellow speeding towards Stoke House, a rum time to go avisiting, unless on urgent business."

She made no comment, but an observant man, he noticed the strain on her face, and wisely ignored it.

"I had a fancy to see the Rectory by night," he said cheerfully, "and a ghostly sight it looks. But your mother's grave, with such delightful flowers, is pleasing. You tend it well, Caroline Mary."

"Thank you," she smiled gratefully and made a hesitant gesture, but thinking better of it, gave a faint shrug and turned away. "If you will excuse me, Mr Borrow, I must return to the Manor. Goodnight."

The black gelding flew across the heath, revelling in the gallop, while his master, with grim determination, spurred him on. Polly's presumptuous words stung like a whiplash. That she had the audacity to accuse him of such greed evoked outrageous indignation. There was no denying she had spirit, indeed it was part of her charm, and the compassion she felt for Arabella showed charity. But never had any woman dominated him, not even Regina, and that chit of a girl with flashing eyes – such wonderful eyes – should not do so now. No other fellow of his acquaintance would tolerate such unseemly wifely conduct, except maybe Hugo Hamilton, who was saddled with the obstinate Lucy.

His thoughts dwelt on the fuss of Arabella's wedding and the air of affluence surrounding Stoke House, which, in his opinion, was largely responsible for bringing her such a splendid match. That much of its luxury was due to Polly's legacy he firmly believed and a fierce urgency to expose such trickery gave him no peace.

Approaching the house where lights were dimmed was no deterrent. If all were abed so much the better, let them wake to learn of the cunning scoundrel, not only they but the whole town. While justice reigned in England it should be done if he made himself a jackanapes in the process.

His thunderous knocking brought Hamilton himself, still dressed and flushed with wine. Hovering on the stairs with startled face was Arabella an excited

Oliver by her side. There was only a moment's hesitation before he dismissed them curtly.

"Go back to bed where you belong, your father and I have business."

He was lead into the study and waved to a chair while a voice boomed in hearty confusion.

"A little late for a social call, but no matter, my boy. Is there something wrong?"

"You may well ask, and the hour has no consequence. But it irks me to discuss serious matters with a drunk."

"I find your insolence offensive," came the heated reply. "I feel a certain justification when indulging my daughter's betrothal to an earl. A little satisfaction from you would not come amiss, at least your conscience can now rest regarding Arabella."

"Conscience? You use a word lightly which must regularly haunt you."

"What riddle is this, Richard? Come to the point, if you please."

"Gladly, and be thankful a fast ride has cooled my wrath. I had a mind to cause you injury." He glanced at the gun-rack ominously. "My question shall be blunt enough to shock you back to sobriety. What became of Rector Wintringham's fortune?"

There was silence in the room but the lamp shone mercilessly on Hamilton's glistening face.

"You do well to cringe," Richard snapped contemptuously, "for Polly's legacy is remarkably overdue, in my calculations. You might wish to deny its very existence and I await your remarks with interest – we have a long night ahead of us."

"Your insinuations are insufferable and deserve no attention. Any client's case is confidential and such a delicate one as this – "

"Delicate! What else has the town to learn about Polly's affairs? She is my wife and nothing can harm her now, I'll request you don't beat about the bush. It is well known the Rector died in Norfolk, the city of Norwich, I believe. Little time is needed to discover if other solicitors were involved."

"There was no other."

"That is as I supposed. I realise most prominent people in this area place their affairs in your hands, Hamilton, and perfectly safe they are, I've no doubt. But I believe one simple girl was easy prey, wealthy but unaware, and I believe the money left in trust for her was used for your own ends. With what incredible ease you could feather your nest, there was no curious partner, and none to enquire of a disliked clergyman best forgotten. Well now, sir, that simple girl is my wife, no longer alone and defenceless. I have every intention of seeing justice done."

The other man with colour now returned, leaned back in his chair. His eyes had a rare glint but his voice was soft as he spoke with dangerous calm.

"I am not a violent man, Sir Richard, otherwise your opening remarks would have seen my servants throwing you from my house. I cannot forbid your defamatory words, but neither can I forgive them, and I have not the slightest intention of satisfying your curiosity regarding the Wintringham estate. You have the insufferable impertinence to accuse me of embezzlement with no foundation whatsoever, and such insults I will not tolerate. But it pleases me to put into words what has been on my mind for some time. You are arrogant, bull-headed and the most self-opinionated young man I have yet to meet and I feel Arabella is well out of your life. I only hope Polly can teach you a little humility."

Richard laughed angrily into his face. "I am not so easily discouraged, neither are my suspicions dismissed." His long arms reached and grasping the other's stock he pulled him forward. "I demand to see a copy of the Rector's will and an account of every penny spent or I'll play the devil with your reputation, by God!"

He was shaking with fury and so incensed that until a sharp voice penetrated his anger another's presence went unnoticed.

"Let him be, Meredith, do you wish a death on your conscience?"

Breathing heavily Richard loosened his grip and sinking into a chair saw Henry Borrow pour three fresh glasses of brandy. Hamilton sipped his nervously but Richard stared moodily at the floor, ashamed of his outburst, yet resenting the intrusion. The newcomer, however, seemed determined to placate them, for he spoke soothingly.

"Far be it for me to interfere, yet I feel your discussion might well be the outcome of my own indiscretion. Am I correct?"

Hamilton glanced up with puzzled eyes, but Richard answered.

"Don't blame yourself, pray. As you know a certain situation has troubled me for quite some time."

"Needlessly, I think, for this unsavoury business has gone far enough – "

The other man, who had sat sombrely silent, snapped, "Do I understand you've been discussing my affairs?"

"Not with hostility, I assure you, John, but isn't it time all the facts were told? Has young Meredith learnt why our partnership ended?"

"There's been little chance of late and at this

moment I'm not inclined."

"So, in spite of many faults, old friend, you still possess unnecessary modesty. But no more shilly-shallying, the story shall be told."

Borrow turned and looked directly into Richard's eyes. "I beg you to listen without comment, fellow, and then be the judge.

"Hamilton and I were partners in this town when Hector Wintringham fled it. True, we believed him a rich man with a granddaughter to inherit his wealth."

"It is just as I thought."

"Oh, no, young man, not as you thought! The Rector was secretive, revealing little to Hamilton or myself regarding his possessions and after his death the will proved worthless. No gold was found, neither did any bank harbour the money we'd imagined. Little enough was forthcoming to feed or educate the child and the man you accuse of fraud provided charitably for her. There was much speculation and we both believed a second will would come to light for everyone's benefit."

"You had cause to think that?"

"It seemed highly probable, for a sealed envelope was attached to the will with strict instructions regarding the contents. Under oath John Hamilton swore the seal remain unbroken until the Wintringham girl's eighteenth birthday. Such a taradiddle seemed nonsense to me and I became impatient, cursing John for a fool at agreeing with the arrangement. The argument it caused was indirectly responsible for dissolving our partnership."

"The Rector had much to answer for."

"To a point, yes. We were younger then, pigheaded and ambitious, and I was mostly to blame for having little use for an unwanted girl. I'd had my fill of small-town gossip and stupid old clergymen and to my detriment chose to practice in London. The Wintringham case dragged on for eighteen years and not a penny piece Hamilton received."

Ashamed, Richard glanced at the sheepish face opposite while the man shifted with embarrassment. Regret at his hasty conduct was gradually ousting the mistrust still vaguely troubling him.

"Polly's birthday was in October, I presume the sealed letter was opened on that date?" he said.

Hamilton nodded. "In London under legal supervision."

"Much good it did you, my friend. The content was merely a scrap of paper containing a rhyme," his ex-partner remarked.

"No clue to the fortune?"

"Regrettably no." Hamilton took a small key from his pocket and opening a drawer in his desk, drew out a paper which he handed to Richard. "Make of it what you will."

The ink and the hand was perfectly clear as he read:

"Wouldst though then remember,
From New Year to December,
Lying midst all seasons' weather,
Heart and head and gold together."

There was silence in the room, and the words drummed in Richard's head.

"It reads like a burial."

"Exactly. Needless to say, the Rector's remains were thoroughly examined and to my deep regret his daughter's grave was disturbed. Fortunately, Polly was in London at that time, for after all these years it was a gruesome business. No possibility could be disregarded, however, although in neither case did we discover gold."

Each man sat quietly wrapped in his own thoughts, and Richard frowned as he broke the silence.

"When Polly first arrived here you took great pains to keep her presence secret. Was there some special reason for that?"

"She was forbidden the county until turned eighteen; it was a condition of the will. But it seemed quite heartless bringing Arabella home and leaving Polly behind for a mere few months. I took the risk over it."

Rising at last Richard stood before Hamilton, his manner contrite. "Can you forgive my poisonous tongue and the actions I sincerely regret, sir?"

His hand was firmly clasped. "Apology is not easy for such as you and 'tis all forgot. Whatever I did for Polly was partly for Arabella's sake, I trust you believe that."

Nodding, Richard turned to Borrow. "Your intervention was most timely, my temper is hasty. I can only hope Polly will so readily understand."

"I don't doubt it, young man, you have a prize worth cultivating there, cherish it. Take the coast road home, it will be to your benefit."

Calmer now, yet still bemused, Richard left the house, his thoughts on the riddle with its perplexing intonations. Were the two men treating him with perfect honesty or would the strange distrust he felt in spite of an affable farewell, persist till the end of his days?"

Mounting his horse, Polly's face, pale and distressed, rose before him and the pressing business of a reconciliation took precedence over all else. He came to the beach, where small waves gently lapped and there she was wandering aimlessly alone. Polly, his beloved, the girl beyond price, life's greatest joy.

As he ran, she turned and saw him splashing over the sand and with arms outstretched and faces aglow they fled towards each other. Lips met stifling apologies and their love was completely absorbing, all problems fading into an unimportant obscurity.

Thirteen

It was the vogue now for brides to wear white, and Arabella had every intention of making her wedding as fashionable as any London one. Her gown of snowy lace exposed plump white shoulders, while elaborate sleeves and the widest skirt possible set every female in the local town agog.

The little church filled to capacity with the bridegroom's relatives, still allowed room for its normal congregation. John Hamilton, puffed with pride, supported Sophia, who despite some misgivings had arisen from her bed for the occasion, while behind them stood Hugo and Oliver. Polly, squeezing Richard's arm, gave Lucy a secretive smile and this was returned with a conspiratorial wink to shock the ladies present. The Caldwell girls, much in evidence, fluttered importantly about the bride and the whole ceremony attracted much comment.

Stoke House, decked with summer flowers, welcomed the guests to a sumptuous feast, and wine flowed freely as with bantering laughter the newly-weds left for London.

Many guests staying overnight continued to imbibe, but Polly and Richard left for the Manor in the soft evening light. They sat together on the driver's seat while the horses plodded home with a lazy indolence.

"A memorable day, without a discordant note," Richard mused. "Hamilton should be proud of his achievement."

"You really are disgracefully biased and give Arabella little credit. She looked quite beautiful today."

"Pleasant enough, I agree, but in a few years I fear nothing will prevent her alarming expansion. Let us hope the fashionable stoutness continues for her sake, but I must say the act of encircling a slender waist gives greater satisfaction, to my mind."

Snuggling closer, Polly laughed as she reviewed the day. No unlikely event happened to mar the service and even Lord Marcelon seemed affected by the tributes bestowed on one of the town's favourite inhabitants. The idea of manually pulling a floral bridal coach the whole way to Stoke House he obviously found gratifying.

It seemed to Polly that her cup was full, the trials and tribulations over. The tale learned from Richard of John Hamilton's generous conduct filled her with shame and humility. She could never atone for her inexcusable behaviour towards him and longed to make amends, but not insensitive to her husband's feelings she played on it as little as possible. Richard still had a slightly cynical attitude towards the whole affair which she did her best to ignore.

The sun set in a burst of glory and Polly noticed how near to the Rectory wall they had wandered. The sad house, contrasting vividly with the one so recently left, found her murmuring to Richard.

"Stoke House is going to be mighty empty. Sophia's no company at all and Oliver returns to school shortly. With Hugo gone and Arabella too, I fear for Mr Hamilton's loneliness. What a blessing he approves of Lucy."

"She's a very sensible girl, and the house on the shore is indeed a credit to her. She intends making a success of her marriage and I must say Hugo exceeds my expectations. But interference from Papa Hamilton will, I'm sure, be unwelcome."

"Oh, I do agree. But, Richard, I wish you would treat him with a little more charity for in spite of everything I feel you still have reservations."

He grinned and tapped her lightly on the nose. "You are a deal too observant for your own good, my dear – "

At the sound of a galloping horse he paused and looking round they both saw a rider thundering directly towards them. Grabbing Polly, Richard leapt from the box as the rider hurtled along.

"He's going to take the wall, by God, oh the fool!"

Collapsing on the ground together they watched transfixed as horse and rider soared gracefully through the air, clearing the high Rectory wall. An almighty crash on the other side sent them racing towards the gates and Polly cried hysterically, "It was Oliver."

They found him lying senseless among the flowers on Caroline Mary's grave but the horse had risen and with frightened eyes was trotting about the wilderness of weeds.

"The young idiot", Richard snapped angrily. "He might have broken his neck and the beast's into the bargain. One of Hugo's new stud, I believe."

"Oh fie to the horse! What about Oliver, is he badly

hurt?''

They laid the boy on the grassy bank while
Richard's expert hands sought for broken bones.

"Simple concussion, I suspect, the flowers
cushioned his fall. He stinks of wine, an unaccustomed
pleasure, I'll be bound, responsible for this prank. The
head he'll carry tomorrow should teach him a lesson –
that and Hugo's wrath, of course.''

Patting the boy's face, Polly looked anxiously at the
still figure.

"He'll not die,'' Richard's voice tinged with
amusement assured her, "in spite of that hellish wall.
We'll keep him in the air for a while, I've brandy in the
carriage.''

Polly, her own colour returning, watched while the
horse was caught, soothed and examined for cuts. She
held the inert hand in her own but relaxed at his
regular breathing, and looked ruefully at her mother's
ruined grave. The low sun gleamed on the headstone
which the horse's hooves had struck with incredible
force and a long score was perfectly visible. Peering
she drew her finger along the deep indentation and
with a shock the gleam of gold caught her eye. A trick
of fading light, and awkward shadow, must be the
explanation and yet fearfully she became aware the
glitter told an undeniable truth.

Staring with incredulity, unwilling to believe it,
Richard's voice, sharp now aroused her.

"Come along, Polly, lift up his head.''

Silently she helped tip the brandy into the boy's
mouth and in a very short time he was coughing and
spluttering, eyes flickering alarmingly.

"We'll soon get you home, boy. Best move him now,
Polly.''

She sat very still and anxiously he asked, "Has the

shock distressed you, my dearest? Rest here a moment while I settle the boy in the carriage."

Thankfully she nodded and watched him disappear. The score mark gleamed now like a finger of light, bringing to her mind a whirl of indecision. Should she keep the secret to herself, the secret of her grandfather's gold. Only she in the whole world had the right to decide and what evil suspicions and still painful wounds might it reopen. She shrank from acknowledging her husband's faults, at suspecting his immediate reactions as with fearful confusion she saw him gently tether the horse.

Returning to her side, the anxiety he showed instantly stilled her quivering body, leaving only the heart beating fast with a single purpose. The strength of their love rested on this venture and only with complete trust could it survive.

When he bent to gather her in his arms her eyes were wet but without hesitation she stayed him, pointing to the scored line of gold without comment.

He stared for a moment before giving a soft awesome sigh, "So it has lain here all these years beneath the humble granite. What a devious man was the Rector to invent such a ruse, but a cruel one to his heirs. This wicked jest was no fitting tribute to either of you.

"Neither to an honest lawyer."

She picked up a gull's feather and smoothed it against her knee, avoiding his eyes, afraid of his words. But his hands took her face between them and turned it up to his own.

"Tell me your deepest thoughts, Polly," he said with ominous quiet.

"Now it is found I want no part of it," she answered slowly, "and I think you know it has always been so."

"For some reason you are fearful and I cannot believe I'm responsible for that. I ask nothing but your happiness and your love, my dearest Polly. The gold has no importance. Suppose we leave it buried here in peace with your mother, a secret known only to ourselves." He touched the shining line in wonder. "Tomorrow no traces will remain, I'll see to it myself."

"Oh, Richard, if you only knew how lately the very thought of it has filled me with disgust."

"I've been aware of many things you tried unsuccessfully to hide. But now it is over and only our life together, without further complications, matters."

He lifted her like a child and her heart full, she lay against his breast. As they left the deserted garden she looked back to see the sombre stone, pale in the twilight, guarding a secret they two shared with only Caroline Mary.

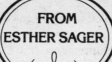